Wind In The Sahara

A Novel

Louise Roberts Sheldon

PublishAmerica

Baltimore

First printing

The characters represented in this work of fiction are entirely the invention of the author, except for a few known public officials whose actions are fictional. Otherwise, any resemblance to persons living or dead is purely coincidental. The circumstances of the Saharan War are true to history and presented as interpreted by the author.

ISBN: 1-59129-620-X
PUBLISHED BY PUBLISHAMERICA BOOK
PUBLISHERS
www.publishamerica.com
Baltimore

Printed in the United States of America

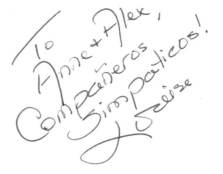

To Anne + Alex,
Compañeros
Simpáticos!
Eloise

Dedicated to my husband Bob

Prologue

He slid away from the truck, shuffling slowly at first, then walking faster. He stumbled over his long garment at the curb. *L'hemdullah!* He must do nothing to attract attention. An unearthly chill coursed through his sweat-soaked body. They could snuff out his life so easily, like batting down a moth on a summer night. He imagined his white *djellaba* smeared with blood and rent with holes.

Mokhtar was a Bedouin. He had never attempted anything like this in his life. Now he had acted against an army of soldiers with an arsenal at their disposal.

He had done what he had to do and he had done it alone. *Inchallah!* With the permission of Allah! If he made it back, he would be welcomed as a hero among his people, the Blue Men of the Sahara. But they didn't call them that now. They had a new name for the freedom-fighters. He had forgotten it. It didn't matter. It was the trembling of his body that bothered him. Even his hands quivered, the very fingers which had pressed into the package the timing device that was to detonate thirty pounds of lethal plastic explosive in precisely ten minutes. He had pushed the package back against the truck's tailgate that faced the open drill ground where it would do most damage.

Leaning down to adjust his flattened slipper, he stole a glance at the Spanish soldiers beyond the wire fence. They thought him some poor peasant driving his produce into town. They took no notice of him. He hated them for that. In the Sahara the Spanish *ejército* treated the Bedouin like the sand beneath their feet. And now they would die for it—many of them.

A horn screeched indignantly into his ear. He jerked his body onto the sidewalk as a huge black Mercedes swept by. Maybe the Governor of Ceuta in a black suit with a clean white shirt was sitting behind those dark-tinted windows. Mokhtar had seen his like in La Ayoun, Spanish colonial officials, arrogant in their tailored clothes and expensive cars. He spat angrily on the pavement. Curses on the Governor and his entire family, for having passed so soon! May they all be bitten by a hairy black spider! Otherwise, they might have seen, even felt, the blast of Mokhtar's inferno.

Five minutes to go. He shivered feverishly through the grimy *djellaba* that clung to his body. He looked back. Spanish soldiers were assembling in front of their headquarters to receive orders. This was how he had planned it, squatting unseen for hours to observe their movements, until he knew the exact moment when the maximum number of uniforms would be massed in one place. This was the focal point, near the immaculate white church and the stone-fronted *ayuntamiento*, where taxes were paid. It was the place for maximum publicity, Bashir had said. Risky as it was, Mokhtar was not going to miss the occasion.

In a stall of the make-shift market that bordered the road, he wedged himself between a pile of yellow melons and tiers of nut-brown cooking vessels. At this early hour there was heavy foot traffic from Morocco across the frontier into the Spanish enclave of Ceuta on the narrow neck of land that connected it to the mainland of Africa and Morocco. Clop! Clop! Clop! A trio of donkeys trotted by, laden with sacks of carrots, followed by several diminutive *Riffi* women in black-pomponned straw hats, their bodies bulging with produce from the fields, and gaunt Moroccan workers by the hundreds, hurrying to degrade themselves by serving the Spaniard.

Mokhtar watched the soldiers, a mass of dark green uniforms milling about the parking lot. Some were smoking and chatting, languidly eyeing the sumptuous Hotel Muralla in front of which a group of Spanish tourists discussed their purchases in this duty-free port. The black hat worn by the detested members of the Guardia

Civil resembled the sooty pot his mother cooked in. A stupid thing to wear on the head at the moment of death!

He glanced at the watch that Bashir had loaned him. Less than a minute to go. Then a gaggle of young women from Morocco, their caftans flapping in the wind, enveloped him. A round, saucy face under a yellow scarf turned toward him, smiling. Then frowning. Was it the livid scar on his face? He lunged to one side, terrified he'd miss the moment. A thought struck him. The women might be hurt, even killed. He felt a pang of remorse.

Then he heard it. The noise had a searing intensity. A wall of thick black smoke was rising, obscuring the marble façade of the hotel, the imposing *ayuntamiento*, even the small white Christian church. Out of the graying cloud a body appeared, sailing upward as if born on the sea wind. It seemed to hover before it crashed clumsily on the pavement. As the smoke cleared, he saw other bodies sprawled grotesquely on the ground. The truck had catapulted meters away and lay on its side. The air was thick with screams and the screech of sirens. Acrid fumes singed his nostrils. The girls had disappeared. An aged Moroccan lay on the opposite sidewalk, his legs stretching awkwardly into the street.

Bashir's warning rang in his ears. "Get out fast. With that scar you could be recognized." Now he moved swiftly but with pride. For he, Mokhtar, fighter for the independence of the Spanish Sahara, was responsible for this act. He had blown to smithereens five, maybe ten, of Franco's soldiers. Spain would blame the Moroccans, and in the Sahara he would be a hero. They were right to have given him their trust, even though he had been trained to fight by the Spanish. He thanked the colonizer for that. Wasn't he known as the surest marksman among the Blue Men?

Mokhtar turned to slip down a side street where Bashir would be waiting. They would hide out for two days, then head for the crowded medina of Tetouan in Morocco. The Moroccans didn't care. They might even take credit for the bombing. They didn't know that Spain would be forced to cede the desert to his people, the Sahraoui. The…the Polisario! That was the new name of the rebel movement.

In August 1975, six Spanish soldiers were killed by a bomb in the Spanish enclave of Ceuta on the Mediterranean coast of Morocco, an incident that set off a chain of events that led to war in the Sahara.

Chapter One

At last the rented Renault bearing Marc Lamont—foreign correspondent, man of the world and *agent extraordinaire*, as he mockingly referred to himself—emerged from a series of rocky outcroppings in a desolate moonscape. Before him, the oasis of Marrakech shimmered in the noon heat like a ship hull-down in the sea. One tower rose above the city's pink ramparts and was outlined against arabesques of date palms and the jagged peaks of the High Atlas beyond.

For a thousand years chains of caravans with their burdens of gold and slaves had snaked over the desert toward these crenellated bastions, he mused. Nowadays, it's the tourists who bring the gold. He sensed a strange elation. Morocco reminded him of his native California—the desert, the mountains, the long sea coast. But this assignment was different, like none he had ever had.

Driving between compact rows of orange trees, he once again felt the visual shock of Marrakech. Unlike the pristine white of other Moroccan towns, its walls glowed with the rich red warmth of local clay. Marrakech not only looked different, it *was* different. A focal point of sorcery and the occult, the southern capital was a legendary center of dissent from the royal mandate in Rabat. And that was the reason for Marc's visit.

Morocco was riding high after its take-over of the Western Sahara, a sizeable chunk of mineral-rich desert. But not everybody agreed with King Hassan that Morocco had the right to annexation simply because of the centuries-old ties between Moroccan sultans and desert

9

tribes. Lately, insurgents in the desert had set up their own government and were waging a war that was daily becoming more of a threat to Morocco itself. Meanwhile, there were indications that sympathetic elements in the south of the country were aiding the rebels.

Marc had been present at the fabled Green March the preceding November when 300,000 Moroccans peacefully crossed the border to take the Western Sahara from Spain.

Now, four months later, he intended to follow up with in-depth digging into dissidence in the south. He was determined to make the Saharan war his story, to stake out this corner of the globe for himself and build an international reputation as a newsman. Thus, he might make up for a few reverses in what, at age thirty-five, was turning out to be a promising but less-than-startling career in journalism. He had always been a charger, dogged in his pursuit of a story, nailing down details with a fury and speed that few other reporters possessed. But he tended to overdo it, to overload the piece, to overwhelm the subject of his writing, as well as the reader. This time he was going to plan his strategy properly, think it through. No alienating of people in the office or in the field. No overlooking possible stumbling blocks. He was going to tread carefully, following the plan he had devised.

At the fabled Hotel Mamounia, his steps echoed through vacant marble halls. Around the pool with its island of palms, empty lounge chairs stretched invitingly and a squad of chefs prepared brochettes and spicy *tagines*. It was high season, but the usual crowd of jet-setters was nowhere to be seen. The war in the Sahara had taken its toll, he thought, scanning the wooden balconies from which Churchill's stubby fingers once captured the blazing colors of bougainvillea and hibiscus. There was a macabre stillness, a sticky sweetness in the golden afternoon.

Three hours later Marc left the hotel, his lean figure clad in his usual garb, blue jeans and open shirt. He crossed the Jmaa el Fna, the city's bustling central square adjacent to the walled medina. The sun's rays now tilted sharply, and a seething populace had begun to stir from its midday lethargy. He passed rows of stalls offering hand-crafted merchandise. Above the crowd, caftans swayed in the wind where once heads of enemy chieftains were displayed. Hawkers touted pyramids of gluey sweets and roasted meats. His nostrils tingled with the sweet and acrid aromas of melting honey, singed mutton and spices like cumin and coriander. He also detected the sickly smell of hashish, momentarily taking him back a decade to his student days at Berkeley.

Marc directed his steps toward Bab Ftor at the edge of the medina. It was the only address the CIA Chief of Station in the Moroccan capital, Rabat, had supplied.

The CIA? Right. That was the new part of his plan—becoming involved with "The Company." They would use his services and he would use them. They paid good money, which would enhance the marginal salary offered by his parsimonious employer, Global Wire Service. More importantly, they had the contacts with key people who knew what was being said and what was being done in the suppressed underbelly of the Moroccan political scene. For a foreigner, or in fact for any reporter, Moroccans included, it was damn hard to get under that tight lid. Underdeveloped countries were inevitably ruled by repressive governments. Furthermore, you couldn't get much out of official sources. Marc's colleagues in Rabat referred jokingly, but quite accurately, to the Ministry of Information as an agency of Disinformation. No one could rely on the thin trickle of doctored news that eked past the creative talents of the palace censors and disinformation experts.

In the Moroccan capital, Rabat, Marc had been boning up for a series of articles on the war in the Sahara when he was contacted by the CIA. With numerous operatives involved in the crises in Beirut and Poland, they claimed to be short of hands. It was fine by him. The job fit in nicely with the story he planned to write on dissidence in southern Morocco. He had been thoroughly screened before his services had been "coopted," as they quaintly put it. And that was it.

"Just ask one of the kids hanging around for Dr. Malki," Dirk McGonigal, the CIA chief, had said. "They know everybody in that labyrinth."

Bab Ftor turned out to be a thick adobe arch, slumped with the weight of centuries, connecting high walls that once encircled the city. To one side of this portal, a venerable seer bent to scrutinize the relative positions of objects on a stool—a bone, a feline claw, a frog's leg, the tail of a rodent. He looked up at the intruder, frowning. Behind him several alleys branched off, reaching like crooked fingers into a dark quarter of the old medina.

"*Fin* Malki? Where's Dr. Malki?"

The old man shrugged. Marc seized the thin shoulders of an urchin and repeated his question. The boy's eyes rolled. Marc knew the game. He fished in his pocket for a dirham and waved two fingers in the boy's face. The child's mouth curled in a sneer. But when Marc spread five fingers, the smudgy face lit up. The deal made, they set off together down a dirt alley, a slit between windowless walls.

"This Syrian doctor better know something," Marc muttered to himself. But his curiosity was stirred. The CIA had been trying to get in touch with a Moroccan agent with whom they'd lost contact. All Marc had to do was to get a message to him. The agent's job had been to infiltrate a group of conspirators allied with the rebel movement in the Sahara. Marc's plan was to exploit the opportunity to break into these circles as well. He intended to use the CIA for his own purposes.

The boy moved swiftly ahead of Marc, wriggling artfully in the half-light past shrouded figures and dark doorways. They took a right, then two lefts, a dogleg following endless blank walls.

"*Hna!*" The boy stopped before a nail-studded door, pounding on the wood with tight little fists. Marc had just tipped five coins into his hand, when he found a pack of urchins pummeling his back and screeching "*Favor!*" He whirled, mustered a ferocious expression, shouted "*Zid!*" and gratefully watched them flee. Just like the flies, he thought, ever-present.

A rattle of bolts revealed a heavy-set man with a short gray-speckled beard that covered the lower portion of his face. For a moment he scrutinized the journalist with a wary eye. Marc explained that he was a reporter covering attitudes toward the war in the Sahara and that the American Embassy had suggested he have a chat with

Dr. Malki.

"Despite your silly politics, I like Americans. Come in." The gray mass parted to emit a Puckish chuckle.

Marc followed the doctor into a large room that seemed submerged in animal skins. Zebra and antelope hides spread from the floor to envelop divans and chairs where an assorted group of men sprawled. Dr. Malki introduced his brothers and nephews. The pale young man with the dark mustache and the embarrassed look was his son Mahmoud.

With a jaunty air, Dr. Malki handed Marc a stack of photographs. He was a musician, as well as a physician, it appeared. Here his rock combo struck a pose, there a busomy singer perched on the doctor's lap. Marc was about to write the man off as an over-age hippy when Dr. Malki pulled him into a small study.

"So what do you want to know?" Tiny points of light twinkled above the thickly matted beard.

When Marc spoke of his intention to investigate the southern tribes, Malki proved knowledgeable, willing to answer questions and make suggestions. But when the newsman breathed the name he had committed to memory, Malki sprang up and closed the door. The braggadocio clown vanished. Dead serious, he looked a different man.

"Why do you come to me about this?" The scruffy eyebrows became question marks.

"I understand you know everybody in Marrakech. Hassan Saadaoui is hard to find," Marc answered evasively. No mention of The Company, of course.

Malki was eyeing him closely, but finally agreed to set up a meeting in the Hotel el Minza in Tiznit for the next evening. If Saadaoui couldn't be there, Malki would leave a message giving the date when a *rendezvous* would be possible.

Marc was still curious about Malki. "Do you mind if I ask where you stand on all this?" he asked casually. "Are you behind the king or the dissidents?"

"Me?" The small eyes opened wide. "I had enough politics already in Syria—which is why I am here. I play my music and stay out of trouble."

The clown act was on again, as Dr. Malki moved with Marc toward the heavy wooden outside door.

Chapter Two

It was dark in the alley when Marc left the doctor's home. He flattened himself against the wall to let a cumbersome donkey-drawn cart pass. As it rattled on, two figures in hooded *djellabas* sprang in front of him. He felt his arms grasped on each side. His reaction was karate-trained, automatic. He wrenched his arms free. His right leg shot out, delivering a swift kick into the crotch of the man on his right, but then he felt his left leg jerked sideways. His head crashed to the ground. As he struggled to rise, the other man was upon him. Turning, he confronted a black face, the lines of the mouth contorted into an unnatural and bizarre smirk. For a moment they glared at each other. Then he seized the hood of the man's *djellaba*, forcing it over his chin. Blinded, the man stumbled, uttering a guttural curse.

Marc bolted, darting around the donkey cart, several pedestrians and burdened mules, hoping that the increasing evening traffic would serve as cover. He was certain that he was moving back along the same route, but was he being followed? When he reached Bab Ftor, he hastened on through the square.

Back in his hotel room, he slumped into a chair, a dripping washcloth on his throbbing head. This was a joke! On the one night of his life when he had treated himself to unadulterated luxury in a world-class hotel, he had had his head bashed in a dark alley. One move for the CIA and all hell breaks loose. Why not just stick to journalism? Always gung-ho for the exceptional story, the break in routine, he had tripped himself up again!

Who were those thugs? Did they have to do with Malki? Or were they simply disgruntled Islamic fundamentalists?

The annoying thing was that his plan for this assignment had been to avoid any and all kinds of trouble. It was high time that he achieve success and stature as a reporter; he needed a series of solid articles to build his reputation at the wire service. After three years with the *San Francisco Chronicle* and four with the *Los Angeles Times*, he was not exactly a greenhorn. He'd had his share of run-ins with editors, like his collision with the mean-spirited nerd who cut his story on illegal aliens. And there had been that glitch with the *L.A. Times* when he was AWOL. Rioting in Watts had broken out again, just when he had gone off to a chalet in the mountains with Vera. That was the lamentable end of his career with the *Times*. He presumed he had learned from the experience. Women had been the cause of a few troubles in his life. Thank God he had remained unattached to any of them.

So why not go overseas? Every reporter coveted a foreign assignment. Marc was fortunate, for his parents were originally from France and he spoke the language like a native. It took real seniority on a daily newspaper, however, to get a plum like Paris. He had signed with the less well-paying Global Wire Service in New York and in two years had landed in their Paris bureau.

There was plenty of work all over Europe. He liked the fast pace, but he wasn't anxious to walk into a beehive of combat. While other reporters in Paris were being sent out to the hellhole that Beirut was becoming, he had asked for the Sahara. He planned to make this desert war his own turf. He had also thought he had drawn the cushy lot, an assignment that would not involve physical danger. So much for that idea!

Remembering his coverage of Morocco's march into what was then the Spanish Sahara, he smiled under the dank cloth. Hordes of unarmed men, clutching copies of the Koran, walking over the border to take a hefty piece of real estate almost half the size of their own country. All this within easy range of Spanish tanks. Because the Spanish dictator, Franco, lay dying, nothing happened. Chalk up one smart move by King Hassan II of Morocco! Marc would never forget the sight of hundreds of thousands of huddled bodies roaring their thanks to Allah across the wind-swept desert.

Now, four months later, the Spanish had withdrawn. Well-armed rebel insurgents, calling themselves the Polisario, were marauding at will, in and out of safe havens in sympathetic Algeria. Morocco with its flimsy air force of seventeen antiquated U.S. F-5s was incapable of standing up to Algeria's hefty armada of two hundred fifty MiG's purchased from the Soviets. The result was a stalemate, with the rebels shooting up anything they wanted to in the Sahara.

Marc's aim was to find out which side the Moroccan border tribes supported and, eventually, how much of a threat the Polisario movement actually posed. For there was long-term U.S. interest in determining whether or not oil-rich Algeria aimed to take over the Western Sahara and further threaten its old enemy, Morocco.

Marc recalled his meeting with Dirk McGonigal. The broad-shouldered CIA Chief of Station, lurching back in his swivel chair, had said in a tone of practiced affability, "You have an interesting file, Lamont. You're tough. You're smart. You have a reputation for going to the end of the line. I like that. You have the languages. You'll do all right."

The CIA wanted to know how vulnerable Morocco might be to incursions by the insurgents, McGonigal continued. The previous year he had recruited a first-rate agent among the Reguibat tribe, long-time trouble-makers in the Sahara. Hassan Saadaoui was razor-sharp, but the agency had lost contact with him.

His voice turned steely. "Your job is to find Saadaoui. Use the recognition signal and give him the message. Here! You can have a look at his dossier and photograph, but no notes. Memorize everything."

It sounded simple enough on the surface. They were a smug bunch in The Company, Marc mused. McGonigal had probably pulled every trick in the game. He also had prestige. If anyone could get in to see the King, it was he. They were somewhat alike, two old toads who had waged many battles.

"How about a gun?" Marc had ventured. He felt foolish the moment he said it.

"Get over the romantic idea that espionage is a James Bond operation!" McGonigal said tersely. "We avoid that kind of trouble. The most lethal weapon you'll get from us is a pen that writes with invisible ink. I'll debrief you when you return."

It was already evening in Marrakech. To avoid having the call traced to his room, Marc used a public phone to call McGonigal at the specified time to the outside number he had been given. According to Dirk, all key telephone lines in Morocco were tapped.

Soon he heard the chief's deep grunt come on the wire.

"I've got the ticket," Marc said, using their code. "No problem at all. The plane will arrive tomorrow." He meant, of course, that the meeting with Saadaoui was on.

"Something has come up that's a little disturbing," McGonigal answered, enunciating the words carefully. "I'm not sure that's a reliable ticket agency. Be careful."

That was surprising. Obviously, he meant Malki. Marc had taken a liking to the doctor.

"By the way, I had a fall on my way back to the hotel. Fortunately, I'm not hurt," he said.

There was no comment on the other end, and Marc hoped that Dirk had some idea of what he was talking about.

"Anyway, I'm off tomorrow morning," he added.

"Good. Get out of town." McGonigal signed off with his characteristic grunt.

Marc didn't like the negative bit about Malki, to whom McGonigal was apparently referring as "unreliable." Also, Marc hadn't mentioned that Aysha was going with him. He had decided that it wasn't necessary. Why complicate matters?

Early next morning he might have been taken for a local garage mechanic, until he stood up. Blue jeans and a slightly muscular frame were not unusual; only his height and sandy brown hair identified him as a foreigner in Marrakech. In a moment his navy blue T-shirt was hunched again under the hood of the rented Renault sedan. He checked the carburetor, fan belt, extra water and, most important, the spare tire. The lug wrench was there, too.

Not that he thought anyone had tampered with the car. It paid to check over these things oneself. He'd had strange experiences in Morocco, as when an out-sized accelerator cord, installed the day before, had brought the car to a standstill in the noon-hour traffic of Casablanca. There would be no mechanics to the south, where the bleak Saharan stretches began.

As he paid his bill at the reception desk, the concierge handed him a message. Several letters in Arabic script were scrawled on a torn sheet.

"Excuse me, what does it say?" Marc asked. His spoken Arabic was limited, but reading was impossible. It was an embarrassing admission.

"*Pardon!*" The concierge looked flustered. "It says, 'Infidel! Leave the Islamic people alone!' There is no signature."

"Thanks," said Marc, whose discolored forehead was still sore to the touch. Dirk was right. It was time to get out of Marrakech.

On his way to the car, he leapt suddenly to one side, fists clenched. As he saw the young man who had tapped him on the shoulder, he smiled foolishly. It was a doorman he had chatted with before lunch. There were so few guests about, his every move was being watched by twenty pairs of eyes, he thought irritably.

"Monsieur Lamont, *pardonnez-moi*." The young man hesitated. "You want to know who left the note?" Marc nodded. "He is dark and heavy. His mouth is so." He twisted his upper lip. "He went very fast to a car in the street. There was a big man with a gray beard waiting for him."

"*Barakallahofik!*" Marc said in thanks, digging into his pocket. Everyone seemed to know more about his business than he did. He pressed a five-dirham note into the boy's hand. The information was worth more than that, but he preferred not to stimulate the boy's imagination. The thought that Dr. Malki might be associated with his attacker was disquieting. The description tallied.

He drove the Renault to the front door, as three porters vied to fetch his suitcase. There had never been so much service at the Mamounia since long before the desert war broke out.

Chapter Three

It was shortly after nine when he left the hotel the next morning. He hoped to be in Tiznit by late afternoon. But first he was to pick up Aysha Larosien, the woman he had met at a party in Rabat the week before. A fellow journalist, Aziz Berrada, had introduced them, claiming that she was the best source on the Sahara that he knew. Anything Marc wanted to know, she would have the answer or she would know where to get it.

Berrada was a close friend. Right away Marc had found this attractive Moroccan congenial and outgoing. Sharp-witted, like most professional men in this country, Aziz knew what was going on at all levels. The only trouble with him was that he had been a member of an opposition party and was thus on the outs with King Hassan despite his aristocratic family connections. *Berrada is an idealist, deeply concerned about human rights abuses*, thought Marc. *In any event, he's one man that I can totally trust in this country.*

He pondered his meeting with Aysha Larosien. Under their dark lashes her strange topaz eyes had surprised him. Confident, almost mocking, they took his measure, leaving him with an oddly unsettled feeling. The eyes of most Arab women he had met gravitated to their feet when confronted by a strange male. "I suppose you are a spy," she said lightly, a hint of a smile implying that he needn't bother to deny it. "I've been anxious to meet one."

"Some people in this country consider every newsman a spy," he parried, relishing the fine-boned structure of her face, framed by long dark hair that fell in a soft curl on her shoulders. *When a*

Moroccan woman is beautiful, he thought, *she is ravishing. This one, even in her trim black European suit, has the proud bearing of an aristocrat.* Impulsively, he asked her to lunch the next day.

It turned out that Aysha, born of a Saharan family, had been brought up in the seaport of Agadir. When that city was destroyed by the earthquake of 1960, she had gone to live with a wealthy uncle in Fez and was educated there at a French *lycée*. She had studied at the university in Rabat and in Geneva. Now she was employed in the Moroccan capital as a translator. She spoke English fluently, as well as French and Arabic.

When he mentioned that he was working on an article on the political positions of the southern tribes, she offered to help. She would be staying with her brother in Marrakech over the weekend and would be glad to introduce him to people influential in tribal politics.

Great! Marc had thought at the time. Berrada had assured him that her background was as she had sketched it and that she was indeed well connected in the south. Now he had second thoughts. Apparently, her contacts were in Tiznit, at least a six-hour drive to the south—perhaps more now that the rainy season had begun. That was where he was to meet Hassan Saadaoui, but things could go wrong with a woman in tow, especially in an Arab country and especially with one he knew so little about.

He swung into the driveway of the villa that belonged to Aysha's brother, Ahmed Larosien, with a slight frown on his face. Aysha was ready. With a sinking feeling, he realized that she was one of the few women who could make a safari suit look seductive. A bright green scarf fell across her shoulders under long, loose hair. She carried a small suitcase. That, at least, augured well.

"Mata-hari in her work-suit?" he jibed, hoping that she wouldn't notice the dark area on his temple near the hairline, a memento of his visit to Dr. Malki.

She laughed, her disquieting eyes confirming the impression of an oriental seductress, as she climbed into the passenger seat.

Slowed by foot traffic, the Renault crawled past the straggling line of rickety shops and *ateliers* that cling to the outskirts of Moroccan towns. Marc shifted into high gear as they moved by the airport onto the open road. They were passing through a grain-producing region where whole villages of squat earthen structures were surrounded by shimmering fields of maize, wheat and barley. Along the roadside, the brilliant yellow blossom of the prickly cactus blazed in the morning sun. And to the left the snow-covered Atlas Mountains rose like a wall holding off the sands of the desert.

Marc listened to Aysha's comments on the regional economy, impressed by the depth of her knowledge. Once again, he sensed the joy of being on the vast continent of Africa. So much of northern Morocco looked like an extension of Europe, but now at last they were approaching the desert which held such fascination for him. As a grammar-school *Beau Geste*, he had strutted on Californian sands and later, in his teens, he had reveled in the exploits of T. E. Lawrence.

Other American enthusiasts of the desert had met misfortune. Two years before, an American diplomat stationed in Rabat attempted to cross the Sahara by car with his family. When the car broke down, he set out on foot to seek help and died of exposure. It paid to keep such stories in mind.

Marc reminded himself that in the Tiznit area he would be dependent on Aysha. That in itself could pose problems. Nonetheless, he had noted that Arab women educated in Europe or America were often as sophisticated and liberated, on the surface at least, as women anywhere. Aysha was no ordinary Moroccan. *En garde*, he warned himself. All I want from her is contacts and background for a series on the Sahara.

They passed through Chichaoua, famous as a regional rug center, took a short-cut by-passing the fishing port of Essaouira on the Atlantic and headed south on a highway parallel to the coast. Marc's throat was parched in the midday heat, and he was grateful that he had decided to stop for lunch at the seaside resort of Agadir, while Aysha rambled on enthusiastically about the city of her birth. She pointed out the kasbah built by the local sheik who drove the Portuguese from their fortress five hundred years ago. Although she had been schooled in Morocco's spiritual and intellectual capital Fez, she seem emotionally attached to languid Agadir with its half-moon beach and its lush plantations of grapefruit and orange trees. After another two hours of driving in what had become a pre-Saharan wasteland inundated here and there with seasonal flooding, she pointed ahead. Like a toy village plunked on a billiard table, the ramparts of Tiznit beckoned through an oasis of palms. Behind its ochre walls a stout tower bristling with protruding beams resembled a grotesque and hairy animal. To Marc, it seemed wholly African, weird yet somehow pleasing.

"The tomb of the Ma el Ainin, hero of the Sahraoui resistance movement!" Aysha said softly.

Sheik Ma el Ainin was a legendary camel rider, a warrior and learned mystic who wrote three hundred works of poetry and philosophy. For a quarter of a century he and his tribe had kept the French out of the desert. During his career he had spawned sixty children by several wives, and so there was no dearth of Ma el Ainin in the area.

"Are you related?" he asked, eyeing the sculptured contour of her profile.

"Indeed I am. You'll meet the present Sheik later today," she said lightly.

So her cousin was the leader of the Ma el Ainin. This was a new twist. Intriguing and useful too—in fact, a gold nugget. But there was all the more reason to stay aloof. If the Ma el Ainin suspected him of involvement with her, his life wouldn't be worth a sou.

Entering town, he followed a series of dusty streets lined with one-room workshops to the faded façades of the main square. A bus lurched ahead of the Renault, halting in a cloud of dust and failing somehow to hit a clump of black goats, tightly roped by their horns. The only other vehicle visible was an oversized Chevrolet from the 50's, looking somewhat worse for the wear. The word "TAXI" was painted in bright blue on the trunk.

The Hotel el Minza was a modest stucco structure, which seemed nonetheless rather grand for Tiznit. Before it, two men tended scrawny donkeys laden with earthenware jugs. Their weather-ravaged faces were topped by black turbans and their indigo robes, hand-dyed in blotches of color, nearly touched the ground.

"My people! The Blue Men!" cried Aysha. "Surely you've heard of the famous camel racers?"

Marc grinned. These people didn't look much like Aysha. He'd seen photographs of the Blue Men on their camels, their long white veils protecting them against the wind. The veil was a good idea. After the long drive in the open car, his mouth tasted dry, gritty and foul.

At the hotel desk, a small man stared blankly at the travelers, his mouth twitching rabbit-like under its mustache. Marc found that neither his French nor his Arabic seemed to make any impression on him. Aysha stepped in, laughing. *Hassaniya*, the Arabic spoken in this region, was different from the northern dialect.

Marc nodded uneasily. Of course he should have realized he'd be at a disadvantage in this part of the world. He had taken a gamble by putting himself in her hands. There seemed to be no problem in getting rooms, however. There were only ten, and they could have their choice.

Marc turned again to Rabbitface, enlisting Aysha's aid. Had anyone asked for him at the hotel? Ayasha translated, enjoying her role. The mustache drooped. No. No one. Marc shook his head. Perhaps Hassan Saadaoui would show up during the evening.

He cheered up upon seeing a roughly hand-lettered sign spelling out in crooked capitals the words, "BAR INTERNATIONAL."

Asking Aysha to order him a Coke, he turned back to the dour little man. Damn it, he'd get through to the fellow on his own. The telephone was essential.

He enacted a charade, listening, talking, listening again, talking. The blank stare intensified and then broke into a tentative smile. The concierge pointed to a door behind the desk.

Marc chortled. The hotel phone even offered privacy. In the cabin he removed the receiver. There was no sound. Returning, he began the sign-language game again. The man nodded happily in agreement.

25

It didn't work. The important point was that it existed. Marc suppressed an urge to take a swing at him.

From the bar, Aysha called, "Sorry, it's the terrible spring rains. There's flooding everywhere. All the lines to Tiznit are down."

Marc cursed. It hadn't occurred to him that there would be no telephone operating out of Tiznit. Now Dr. Malki couldn't get in touch with him in case Hassan Saadaoui was unable to make the *rendezvous*. He walked into the bar, wondering if this was going to be one of those assignments in which everything slipped out of control. Undismayed, Aysha regaled him with tales of the region. He was aware that, for the moment at least, he was glad of her company.

An hour later, Marc and Aysha were joined by a young male of the Ma el Ainin tribe. Chaperon, guide or henchman, or more probably all three rolled into one, Marc surmised. They drove to a house on the outskirts of town where, framed in the doorway, a man waited. The hood of his diaphanous white robe was drawn about his face, emphasizing its almost girlish beauty. Aysha introduced him as the poet Abdelaziz Ma el Ainin, the present sheik and leader of his tribe. The sheik bowed his head, whistling their names softly between fine, white teeth. Marc could not help but note the resemblance to Aysha.

Several male cousins waited in a large salon, where an orgy of reds, oranges and yellows blared from carpets and sofas. Against this typically Berber backdrop, the Sheik Ma el Ainin appeared more gauzy and seraphic than ever. He motioned to his guests to sit down.

Then in a shrill voice, he began a long discourse which, because of the sheik's educated Arabic, Marc was able to grasp the gist of. Behind the colonizer, a chill wind sweeps the desert, he said. When Morocco achieved independence from the French in 1956, revolt was everywhere in the south. Now again, tribal rivalry had intensified since the Spanish withdrawal from the Sahara. Fierce enmity had sprung up between the Ma el Ainin, who were loyal to the king, and the Reguibat, whose warring and pillaging were well-known. The Reguibat had joined forces with the Polisario rebels in the desert and now their combined forces were receiving from Algeria what the Spanish never gave them—guns and ammunition.

"Above all," the Sheik warned, "beware of the Reguibat."

Abruptly, he clapped his hands. In response, two dark-skinned servants appeared carrying a steaming tray. It was the *mechoui*, the young lamb of the desert, served whole with the sweet rice of the Sahraoui. Conversation stopped as the clan gathered up their robes to squat tightly around a low table of chiseled brass. Marc closed his note pad. Food in this country was more important than talk, and he didn't wish to appear impolite. He concentrated on pulling piping hot morsels from the carcass and navigating them to his mouth with his right hand, while keeping his left hand immobile in his lap. As he well knew, its use, reserved for other physical necessities, was taboo while eating. Eyeing him from across the table, Aysha suppressed her laughter. He grinned. The lamb was succulent.

"So the Ma el Ainin back Morocco, and the Reguibat have gone over to the enemy," said Marc later, as they returned to the car.

"More or less. You'll get to meet the other side, too." Her glance was almost mischievous.

Okay, he thought, *she is well connected*. But she still surprised him. Her lifestyle seemed hardly fettered by Muslim law.

"It didn't bother you coming with me and dining alone with the men? I mean, as a woman?" he asked clumsily.

"Not really. They are my family, and our ties are strong. In the desert, girls are educated with the boys. The woman is mistress of the tent and mistress of herself." She looked at him straight in the eyes. Her voice had cooled. He realized that there was a steeliness about her. She was no pretty little thing. She knew her own mind and she knew her own people.

He shrugged. He was grateful to her. The evening had been worthwhile. In fact, it would make great copy. Now he wanted to get back to the hotel to see if Hassan Saadaoui had shown up.

Chapter Four

The concierge produced his Chaplinesque smile, the mustache curving into a pleasing bow. This time he had good news. A man had asked for "Monsewer Lamont." He was waiting upstairs. Marc beamed at his erstwhile tormentor. To insure his visitor's privacy, he had left his door unlocked.

Then something strange happened. Having translated for Marc, Aysha was now involved in an angry exchange with the concierge. Flushed, she turned on Marc.

"Someone for you? Why? Who arranged it?" Her eyes smoldered as if he had played some sort of trick on her.

"I was expecting someone. That's all," he said as they mounted the stairs together. It was an odd reaction, he thought. It was the first time he had seen her lose her sophisticated detachment.

Impatiently, he pushed open the unlocked door to his room and switched on the feeble ceiling light. He had the impression that he had entered the wrong room. Somebody was on the bed. Otherwise, the room was as bare and cell-like as when he left it. A man in Moroccan clothing, who appeared to be in his forties, was sprawled on the bedspread. Was his visitor asleep? Then Marc saw the neat round hole, and beneath it a dark red pool saturating the sheet. He noted that there were no signs of a struggle. The man had been shot in the temple in a highly professional way.

Suppressing the wave of nausea that rocked him, Marc slipped his hand into the pocket of the *djellaba* and pulled out a worn identity card bearing a photograph of the corpse. Below it, the name Hassan

Saadaoui was printed in Arabic and French.

Dirk McGonigal's missing agent had found him! Questions flooded his mind. Who besides Malki knew that Saadaoui was coming here? What could have marked him for assassination? Hassan Saadaoui had not been working for the CIA for several months. Nonetheless, the killing could be a warning to the CIA, since he was meeting an American.

Either they simply wanted him dead or they wished to prevent his making contact with the Americans. Or was Marc merely being scared off? There were myriad possibilities. What a blow this would be for McGonigal, who thought so highly of Saadaoui!

Now he really needed Aysha's help. He knocked urgently on her door.

Her horror at seeing the dead man was genuine.

"Oh, my God! Who is it?" she asked softly. She was looking at Marc with an expression he had never seen. Fear? Distrust?

"I don't know him," Marc said. "Just wait. Don't make a sound!"

He brushed by her to check the other rooms down the hall. One door was unlocked and the room was empty. In the hall bathroom he found a towel, which he wound tightly around the dead man's head.

"I had nothing to do with this. You know it," he said brusquely.

"How do I know it? I don't!" she rasped, firmly closing the door to the hall. "But you can't bring in the police. I have to trust you."

He gave her a hard look. Why was she so concerned?

"You're right," he said. "I want the body out of here before someone pins it on me. I haven't a chance in this place as a foreigner." He spoke quickly as he worked. "Here, help me lift him. We'll get the police on it later."

Aysha nodded. She seemed stunned, yet somehow relieved. Did the involvement of the police worry her more than the murder itself? He had no time to ponder. Together they lifted the body, swathed in the bloody sheet, and carried it to the empty bedroom. It was an act of God that the bleeding was checked.

"Someone wants to implicate me in this—you see, I was supposed to meet this man," he said slowly. "I intend to find out who wants to frame me, without getting thrown in the local jail. We need to know if anyone else has been in the hotel since we left." For a moment he wondered whether she would cooperate.

She said simply, "Yes. I'll go down at once."

Her mood had changed again. The hostile front had disappeared as quickly as it came. Apparently still in shock, she wasn't going to ask questions about Hassan Saadaoui. Relieved, he locked the door with his own key and followed her downstairs.

The concierge's post-midnight smile was thin. Everything was all right? Did his friend find Monsewer?

No, not exactly, he must have gone away. Aysha passed it off lightly, questioning him casually. Marc caught most of the exchange. No one had asked specifically for him. Yes, there had been another man in the hotel during the evening, inquiring about its occupants.

"Get details!" Marc hissed. "Who was the guy snooping around?"

The rabbit nose behind her jiggled with silent laughter.

"He says, a blond man with curly hair, not very tall, French. He wears white pants, very tight." Aysha was visibly shocked.

The description fitted a well-known French fashion designer in Marrakech. Marc had stopped by his boutique at the Mamounia Hotel.

Now he seized Aysha's arm. "Louis Bertrand! Do you know him?"

"He's a *couturier*. I've modeled for him. That's all I know." She seemed genuinely bewildered.

The sharp eyes of the concierge had not missed the exchange. They now focused on Marc's fingers as they removed two ten-dirham notes from his wallet and laid them on the counter.

"Tell him I want to know anything at all he might know about this Frenchman. How did he get here?"

All smiles now, the concierge told them that the Frenchman had come with the taxi, the one in the square.

"Where's the driver?" asked Marc, heading for the door.

Across the square the dilapidated Chevrolet occupied its place of honor as the only available motorized conveyance in town. Marc took a careful look at the pudgy body slumped in the driver's seat. This one was definitely alive and snoring peacefully.

Aysha spoke sharply, jarring the man awake. A five-dirham note thrust through the window caused him to sit up and rub his eyes dolefully. Nonetheless, he soon managed mumbled answers to Marc's volley of questions.

The blond Frenchman, it seemed, had hired the taxi through a local fisherman to come to the coast to pick him up and take him back again. He kept a boat off the beach. A large white motor boat. The man was a great tipper! Were they friends of the wealthy Frenchman?

"Sure," said Marc expansively. "How about taking us to the boat now?"

Aysha nodded her agreement.

The driver uttered an anguished bleat. In the middle of the night? Did they have any idea of the state of the road? There were wash-outs, lakes of water to cross.

"Just tell him to take us. I'll pay double for the return." Marc waved a fifty-dirham note. The driver's lips remained set in an obstinate pout, until Marc pulled another twenty-five from his wallet.

The driver had not exaggerated. The road to the coast was washed out in many places, causing the car to zig and zag a crazy course. Several times Marc clutched Aysha to keep her from cracking her skull against the roof. Although it seemed an eternity, it couldn't have been more than ten miles when they passed a shrine, its dome glowing spectral white in the moonlight.

"Sidi Moussa d'Aglou," the driver said, answering Marc's question. "It's empty. The hermit is dead. The beach is very near."

"Lights out!" Marc snapped.

The car lurched onto unpaved track, its wheels whining for a minute in a sea of mud, as they approached an open space. A three-quarter moon created a bright path on the rippling expanse of water ahead, interrupted only by the dark silhouette of a cabin cruiser, which at the moment carried no lights.

Asked how many men he had seen on the boat, the driver shrugged. Probably only two. He had taken one in the car.

Marc scanned the beach. Seizing a stick, he poked at thickets along its rim. Shortly he stumbled and almost fell into a light fiberglass skiff that was hidden well above the tide mark. Of recent manufacture, it had to belong to the cabin cruiser. Local fishermen used heavy wooden boats. If the skiff was on the beach, at least one of the men was ashore. He could handle the other. Marc returned to Aysha. Her face looked pale in the moonlight.

He put a hand on her arm. "I appreciate your coming. Please stay with the driver and keep on the look-out. In case of trouble, get help in Tiznit."

There was no other way to do it. Mechanically, he blessed his father, who had trained him early in a round of sports, involving survival techniques and self-defense. He supposed that for a newspaperman he was in reasonably good shape. He dragged the skiff to the water's edge, murmuring a prayer of thanks. The oars were in it and the surf was light. With quick, short strokes he rowed toward the cruiser, following the moon's path, which was fortunately not visible from the cruiser in his direction. Resting his oars, he came up silently under the stern. He heard no sound other than the gentle slap of the waves under the ship's hull.

He raised his head above the gunwale and noted a dim arc of light glowing from the cabin window. Gently, he hoisted himself aboard and peered down the open hatch, trusting the waves' rhythmic beat to cover the sound of his movements. The thin strands of blond hair spread over the pillow and the craggy young-old face could not be mistaken. It was the man he had seen at the Mamounia.

Marc pulled gently at the cabin door. He couldn't budge it. He watched Louis Bertrand stir in his sleep and roll away from the light. Then he eased his angular frame up, over and down and through the hatch, groping with his feet for the ladder. At that moment Bertrand awoke and started to rise.

"*Zut alors! Qui êtes vous?* Who are you?" he managed to get out before Marc dropped squarely upon him, knocking him prostrate. In a second his arm was wrapped around Bertrand's neck.

"Why did you murder Hassan Saadaoui?" he barked in French, then English.

"Let me go!" the Frenchman gasped hoarsely.

Marc pressed his arm muscle against Bertrand's Adam's apple, repeating the question.

"I did not murder Hassan Saadaoui!" Bertrand sputtered.

"I know you were in the hotel in Tiznit tonight. Who are you working for?"

Marc's fury was barely controlled. *Careful*, he admonished himself. He had almost killed a judo student once.

"Who *are* you working for?" he hissed again. His jaw jutted belligerently above the older man. "Where are your papers?"

Bertrand's face turned a mottled purple. Red veins swelled in his eyes.

"Let me go, *imbécile!*" he choked. "We're in the same game on the same side." In the faint light he looked tired, much older than Marc had thought.

Marc's answer was to shake Bertrand violently. He spoke through clenched teeth. "Same game? I'm not a killer. You damn frog! You'd have been the first!"

"Fool! Calm down or you'll kill someone on your own side one of these days. I'm with SDECE, French Intelligence." The forced admission came in a barely audible whisper.

"Damn you! Why did you kill Hassan Saadaoui?" Marc asked weakly.

Bertrand sat up with an effort. "I didn't. I was going to meet him tonight. He was working for us until you came along. You're CIA, right?"

"I'm a journalist," Marc said, knowing it was useless to deny the agency connection. "Saadaoui used to work for the Americans."

"I know. But we took him over."

Marc felt his hackles rise. The French thought they had a monopoly on the country. "Prove you're with SDECE!" he countered.

"You must be new to this trade. I don't carry those credentials on me any more than you do. You're going to have to believe me." Louis Bertrand rubbed his neck ruefully. Straightening his rumpled shirt, he got up and put a kettle on the stove.

Marc relaxed warily, aware that Bertrand was probably telling the truth. He watched the Frenchman prepare two mugs of coffee, pouring a generous dose of cognac in each.

"Are you certain that Saadaoui was killed?" Bertrand asked in a strained voice.

Thoroughly shaken by the news, he did not, however, seem concerned about the Moroccan authorities. He was on good terms with the police chief at Sidi Ifni down the coast, he said. He'd take the boat down there right away, clear Marc of any involvement and get the Moroccans working on it.

Marc's eyes narrowed. So Bertrand would dispose of the corpse, in fact take care of everything. It just might serve the purpose of French Intelligence to get rid of the body before the Americans started asking questions.

He turned sharply to the Frenchman. "If you're lying, Louis, I'll find my way back to you."

He knew he had to take the chance that Bertrand was leveling with him. He had to trust somebody. He had something else on his mind now—the attack in Marrakech. He had a feeling that it was no routine mugging. Did Bertrand know about a dark-skinned Moroccan thug with a hairlip?

Bertrand whistled. "Oufkir! We know him well. Oufkir is number one on my list. Does the name ring a bell?"

It was Marc's turn to stare. The Security Chief who had engineered the aborted coups of 1971 and 1972. The fabled Oufkir! Marc had read of the massacre at the king's birthday party, when nearly one hundred guests were shot by army cadets at the summer palace at Skhirat. Oufkir was also responsible for the failed attack on the king's private plane the next year.

This was the nephew of the infamous Security Chief, Bertrand explained, pouring himself an extra dollop of cognac. The French had him tagged as a terrorist trained by the Cubans. He worked for the Algerians all over Morocco and passionately hated King Hassan II. The murder of Hassan Saadaoui sounded like Oufkir's work, and Bertrand made clear that he was eager to get busy on it.

There was a shout from the shore. Louis Bertrand unlocked the hatch and brandished a flashlight with wide arm swings. It was his man, looking vainly for the skiff. He had been let off to visit his village because it was to be a quiet night, Bertrand said with a sardonic chuckle.

Through a porthole Marc saw that daybreak was not far off. Thank God, Aysha had the good sense to keep quiet. He decided to tell Bertrand about her.

The Frenchman smiled. "Tell Aysha anything you want to invent about this encounter. Just don't tell her who I work for. Understood?"

"You haven't got anything on her, do you?" Marc interjected.

"No, not yet. She travels a lot and has some strange friends. I watch her just like I watch everybody else," Bertrand answered.

Just like the CIA, thought Marc. *A chimera in every corner!* Still, he was glad they didn't have anything on her. He climbed through the hatch and hauled in the skiff.

"Before you charge off again, let me tell you something." The Frenchman's lined face, appearing from the hatch, reflected his fatigue. Two weeks before, an American free-lance newsman had driven over the border into the desert with two French reporters and a photographer, he said. They were after stories in the war zone, thought they'd find the Polisario. But they had simply disappeared. They could have been shot by either side or, of course, become lost in the desert. The Moroccans didn't authorize such junkets.

"*Ecoutez,* Marc," he continued, "the longer you're in this game, the more you learn not to take chances! The Sahara is No Man's Land. Don't forget it!" Bertrand gave the skiff a hearty push toward shore as Marc picked up the oars.

A pre-dawn glow bathed the eastern sky in light tones that contrasted sharply with the dark water behind him. The sun rose over the land here, as it did in California, he noted. It was a good sign. A cooling breeze sent a tingling sensation along his scalp, and Marc felt strangely elated. As he neared the beach, Dirk McGonigal's words reverberated in his head: "No flaps, don't involve the police, just do your job."

His job was to find Hassan Saadaoui. The man was dead. Bertrand would take care of the body. So he was free to do what he had set out to do—infiltrate the southern tribes that were dealing directly with the Polisario. Aysha had promised a meeting with "the other side." That meant the Reguibat, the hated enemy of the Ma el Ainin. The story would be dramatic.

He had something else to do, too, a personal score to settle. He would have preferred that McGonigal had supplied him with a gun— if only for self-defense—because he would be on the look-out for Oufkir. He wanted to find him before Bertrand got to him.

Chapter Five

The narrow belt of road stretching south hugged a rocky outcropping of the Anti-Atlas mountain range, traversing a sandy plateau too poor to support beasts of burden. Here a lone man struggled with a wooden plow, there a woman lifted her water jug near a rare clump of flowering oleander. The Renault ascended into terrain strewn with great boulders where only the argane tree pushed its claw-like roots into the ground. Above their gnarled trunks, goats clambered among the branches to munch the thorny leaves. *Sure-footed devils*, thought Marc, *their sharp little hooves never slip.* He'd like to be as sure-footed. Beneath them a ragged goatherd shrieked furiously at the passing car.

Marc felt exhilarated by the events of the previous night—the meeting with the Ma El Ainin and the clash with Bertrand, which revealed much about French involvement in Moroccan politics— and the prospect of interviewing members of the notorious Reguibat clan. Immediately he sobered, thinking of the loss of Hassan Saadaoui, apparently a very good man and a key element of the puzzle he was determined to decipher.

And then there was the aftermath. Marc had stopped with Aysha in the hall to admire the fine filigree of the hand of Fatima that hung from her neck. He had laughed. She seemed the last person to need this sign of Allah's protection. She entered her room, and he followed the movement of her lithe body under her loose caftan. For a moment, he hesitated, remembering the sight of the corpse on the bed in his room. She switched on the light and closed the door behind him. In one swift movement her caftan was over her head and flung in a heap on the floor. Except for the hand of Fatima on its golden chain, she stood naked before him. Her skin was the color of honey, her breasts round like the melons of the Rif, her hips wind-sculpted dunes of sand. He moved toward her and in the rush of their embrace, all thoughts of Oufkir and the rest evaporated into the stillness of the early morning hour.

Now, with the sun high in the sky, he glanced at the composed face beside him. Aysha was an island unto herself. The passion of a few hours ago, the warmth, the wild enthusiasm of their love-making that he knew she had shared with him, had not lessened her self-possession. Under her veneer of European culture, there were hidden layers of another, centuries-old tradition that taught women to hide their emotions and their vulnerability, and to trade instead on their cleverness and their ability to manipulate others. To a Westerner, she was an enigma; there was something unconquerable about her.

Seeing her cryptic smile, he remembered tales of powerful potions possessed by women of the desert. There were stories of French explorers and Legionnaires, smitten lovers who never cared to return to Europe. Damn it! A love affair with Aysha clashed with the dictates of common sense. *Back off*, he warned himself.

They were to meet Aysha's contact "on the other side" at Bou Izakarn, which turned out to be a cluster of nondescript shacks huddled among tall shafts of eucalyptus, whose scant foliage provided little relief from the blazing sun. At Aysha's bidding, he stopped the rented car in front of a sun-faded sign advertising Orange Crush. While she entered a café to use the telephone, he pondered the bleakness of the scene. A wizened female wrapped in drab indigo scurried by. A group of turbaned males slumped against the café wall, looking patriarchal, as if cast in stone, reminding him that in this fierce wasteland, youth seemed to be burned out before adolescence. Aysha emerged in her light safari suit, the scarf fluttering through her black hair. Where did she fit in this desert picture? In this sweltering village she looked as out of place as a Paris model.

Here they would turn off the main road onto dirt track, she said.

They were to meet her people in Ifrane, a deserted town in the hills to the north. Centuries before Mohammed founded Islam in the Arab world, there had been great battles between Jews and Christians in the region, and the Jews had stayed. Recently, they had abandoned the mountain village to emigrate to Israel, and thus today the place ensured privacy.

The fiery sun that follows the spring deluge had baked deep craters into the road, causing the car to bounce from rut to rut as it slowly climbed. Marc cursed silently. With only a single spare tire, he could soon be in trouble. He wondered about her "contact," what she meant by "the other side." Why hadn't she wanted him to call the police in Tiznit?

"I presume you've set us up in a five-star hotel," he quipped brightly.

"Not exactly," she said. "You won't find an American bar."

"Don't pull that on me! You seem to enjoy an occasional swig from the flask," he rejoined, glancing at her.

"It wouldn't do here," she said, staring down the road.

In the barren wilderness she appeared to have discarded her cordial, open manner. He was uncomfortably aware that he had no idea what thoughts, what emotions lay under her lacquered surface. Certainly she enjoyed being the one who pulled the strings.

"Stop here!" Aysha said abruptly, as they approached a low wall paralleling the road.

Beyond it, adobe dwellings sprouted like dark mushrooms, a stream flashed among irregular patches of iridescent green. Among the huts a wooden beam with its bucket made a triangle over a well. It seemed a tranquil retreat.

Marc locked the car, leaving their suitcases, and followed Aysha as she led the way to a hut at the far side of the village. Softly she called into the dark interior and stepped inside, beckoning to him. He followed warily. The moment he moved out of the blinding sunlight, he felt himself seized from behind. He leg shot out in a practiced karate kick, but his arms were already pinned behind him. From the side someone was slapping his legs and thighs, testing for firearms. It might have been a bad dream. It was just as well about the gun, he thought, remembering Dirk McGonigal's admonition.

Mustering his strength, he jerked his arms free and received a blow on the head that sent him reeling to the ground. A hand on his neck held him face-down. He felt hands groping in his pockets. The key to the Renault, his passport, his wallet and the identity card issued to registered journalists by the Moroccan Ministry of Information were swiftly removed.

"He's all right," Aysha was saying in Arabic. "He's harmless." She turned to Marc, speaking French. "Sorry! They don't know you. They think it's necessary."

Marc groaned. Throbbing pain beat a heavy rhythm from the top of his head. Dry dust clogged his nostrils, but his eyes had adjusted to the darkness. A stocky man in dark pants and T-shirt was engaged in a bitter exchange with Aysha.

"They're willing to talk as long as you're tied up," she said. She shrugged her shoulders as if to disassociate herself from the business.

A tall man clutched him from behind. A short burly one with a distinct facial scar was tying his wrists together with a stout thong. The man behind him propped him up in a sitting position.

Marc felt rage boiling within him, as his eyes sought Aysha's. The bitch. The treacherous little bitch!

"They're from the other side," she said coolly, averting her eyes. "They'll explain."

Two other men in *djellabas* and turbans sat by the wall. One of them was older than the other; a coarse gray beard had grown well below his face. They were scrutinizing his passport, the cards in his wallet. The two thugs who had worked him over moved outside.

"Who are you? Why are you detaining me?" Marc spat out the words.

"You're American?" The younger of the two by the wall spoke in heavily accented French.

"I am a journalist from the United States of America," Marc said, crossing his legs under him on the hard earthen floor. He felt ridiculously unimpressive in his dust-covered jeans. His shirt had been torn in the scuffle and his hair was matted with sweat and dirt. "More likely a spy from the Central Intelligence Agency." The grating jeer hung in the dusty air.

"You have my documents in your hands," Marc snapped.

"The United States does not support our cause." The older man sounded more reasonable. He held up Marc's passport to verify the resemblance to the photograph. "We represent the Saharan Arab Democratic Republic," he said, slipping Marc's passport, wallet and key within the ample folds of his *djellaba*.

"I've never heard of it!" Marc glared at Aysha, who had moved to the window, her back to him

The younger, round-faced man spoke up in untutored but well-rehearsed French. They were a nation of one million people, whose manifesto proclaimed autonomy for the former Spanish Sahara. The new Socialist state, led by Secretary-General El-Ouali Mustapha Sayed, included all who would fight for freedom.

"I have heard of the Polisario Front," Marc said in a conciliatory tone. "In fact, I came here to learn more about it." He had succeeded in controlling his anger, and he now noted Aysha's embarrassed look which seemed to indicate that she hadn't planned it this way. However, he had no choice but to go along with them for the moment. And he definitely wanted to know more about this "new republic," whatever it might be.

The older man moved closer. As he spoke, his French revealed the benefit of some education. After the illegal Moroccan invasion and the withdrawal of the Spanish, he explained, two thousand Sahraoui troopers dropped from the Spanish army had crossed over to Algeria to join the Polisario. They were strong now. They had founded a new state and would fight to get their country back.

You bet, Marc thought. The American ambassador had warned King Hassan that the former Spanish troops, well-trained fighters by desert standards, would cause trouble in the Sahara. He had tried to convince the king to take them into the Moroccan army.

"It is the Reguibat who make the Polisario strong," the younger man crowed. "The Reguibat are the 'Sons of the Clouds,' 'Masters

43

of the Desert'!"

Marc grinned. He had finally met up with that infamous tribe. These characters would make terrific copy. He tried another tack.

"*Hablan Ustedes español?*" he asked. "If you're from the Spanish Sahara, you must speak Spanish!"

"We refuse to speak the language of the colonizer!" the older man interjected curtly.

Marc chuckled. They spoke French readily enough which would seem to prove that they were Algerian Reguibat from the former French colony.

"He mocks our cause!" the young man growled and went into a huddle with the older one.

Marc was pleased that he had put them on the defensive. He twisted his torso toward Aysha, for it was high time to find out where she stood.

"Let me talk to the American," she said and seated herself beside him. "First you met the Ma el Ainin who support Morocco. Now you hear the voice of freedom for my people." She might have been explaining the elements of logic to a schoolboy.

He stared at her, dumbfounded. She admitted to being one of them!

Aysha lowered her voice. There were only two sides. In the desert, the fuzzy gray area he sought did not exist. There was the black of night, the white of day; one had to choose.

He might learn something from an ancient Berber fable concerning two beetles named Justice and Injustice. One day Justice set out with her friend Injustice on a trip through the desert to the tomb of a saint. On the way, Justice ate up all her provisions, while Injustice saved food for the return trip. When Justice became famished, Injustice offered her hungry friend a meal, in exchange for an eye. Justice agreed that it was better to lose an eye than to die; later, almost starved, she gave up her other eye. To this day, Justice wanders blind in the desert.

"A nice story. Sounds like Aesop," Marc said. The story described his present circumstances more than he cared to admit.

He cursed his gullibility. He was the blind one! By assuming that Aysha supported the Moroccans, he had allowed himself to be led into this trap. He struggled to control the slow fury kindling again within him.

"You have done well to speak of blinding, Aysha," the older Reguibi said decisively. "I do not trust the American. He doesn't understand our cause. We'll take him to the camp and let El-Ouali deal with him. We can't let him go now. He could be a spy. Anything he reports will be negative."

A shudder shot down Marc's spine. Now he was to be carted off to Algeria, trussed like a helpless bird. He glared at Aysha.

"They'll give you a medal for this! By Christ, you deserve it!" he spat out.

Her eyes looked through him. "Why do Americans think they are untouchable? More special than other people?"

Damn the cold bitch! She really *was* one of them!

The two guards came in. The stocky man jerked Marc's body erect, while the other tied a black cloth around his head. In a few moments they were gone. He was left alone with his morbid thoughts in an abandoned hut on the edge of the Sahara. He had fallen for the scheme of Aysha, a woman he thought was working with him. She had simply turned the tables. She had aroused his passion, outwitted him, duped him. She was a Polisario agent herself! His resentment welled up against her rather than against his guerilla captors.

He shifted his legs to a more comfortable position, and his anger gradually cooled as he began to see things in a more rational light. His predicament was hardly hopeless. In fact, things might be working out rather well. So he *was* trussed up! Ignominious as hell, yes, but the injury was to his pride more than anything else. This was one way—and perhaps, at the moment, the only way—to get into the Polisario camp and meet their leaders. An interview with the Secretary-General would be a world-first!

His ironic laugh resounded as his thoughts charged down this new alley. Aysha might have done him a favor. Perhaps, in her devious way, this was what she had intended. Typically, his anger had erupted, blotting out reason. He had flailed at them all. Sometimes he regretted his outbursts of temper, for it was more difficult, and sometimes impossible, to backtrack and make amends.

Damn! he caught himself up. *Who are you trying to please anyway!*

Chapter Six

It was the time of high heat when the people of the desert sleep The air was oppressive. Seated cross-legged in the hut, Aysha had been absorbed in a book the Sahraoui had taken from Marc's suitcase. Now she began to read aloud in halting English: "'Arabs could be swung on an idea as on a cord...till success had come, and with it responsibility and duty...then the idea was gone and the work ended in—ruins.' Ha!" She broke off, turning petulantly to Marc.

"What bigotry! He's insulting!" She slammed the paperback on the earthen floor.

"T. E. Lawrence knew the Arabs. Actually he was very partial to them. I'm glad I brought it along." His smile below the blindfold betrayed his relishing the thought that the book had touched a sensitive area, puncturing her armor.

"He compares the Arabs to your sterile Anglo-Saxon culture! It's meaningless! We have a great history, we have a great literature. The beginning of civilization occurred in the Arab world." She pushed aside the empty plate of food that she had brought him.

"You think the Polisario state won't survive!" she said after a pause, tracing a tentlike contour in the dirt.

"If they had to go it alone, they wouldn't have lasted this long," he said bluntly.

"You underestimate our people!" She seemed on the defensive, aware and perhaps embarrassed that she had lured him into a trap.

He had continued his positive line of thinking during the last hour or two. With a visit to the Polisario camp, he could pull off a veritable scoop. No American had been there. Possibly, the only way to get there was as a prisoner. He would get the answers he needed first-hand, from the horse's mouth—from El-Quali himself, Grand Khan of the new republic! By God, he'd make his mark as a journalist with this story. He hoped that darkness would fall soon so that they could start for the desert.

"By the way, thanks for the brochettes and for convincing them that I needed a stretch," he said more kindly. She had been that thoughtful. He could starve as far as the rest of them were concerned.

She wiped the perspiration from his forehead.

"Why are you doing this?" he asked. What a strange woman she was!

"Drying your forehead?" she asked languidly.

"Yes, that," he laughed. "And working for the Polisario." He didn't get it. Didn't it split her loyalties down the middle? After all, she had been brought up in Morocco.

She shook her head. She loved Morocco. It was her country. But she believed in a new order, born in the desert, that would eventually sweep over the entire country. Was he aware that half the Moroccan population was underfed, living well below every established poverty level? To buy food, peasants in arid areas were forced to sell the fertilizer that the government distributed to them. The super-wealthy one percent were meanwhile investing their fortunes abroad. Sycophants of the crown were inundated with generous gifts, automobiles and fancy villas to insure their loyalty to the king. The new progressive state would do away with this rich elite and all the other old inequities. Marc would understand when he visited the Polisario, for the freedom-fighters believed passionately in their cause.

An hour ago I could have whipped her, Marc thought. *But she believes what she's saying. She truly wants me to see the camp and talk to them. That much is genuine.*

"What I'd really like to know is how you get away with so much. Like being here alone with me now?" he asked quietly. She still had a lot to explain.

"In the SADR, Sahraoui women share responsibility with men. I can do what I please. I outrank the four of them, except perhaps Rachid, the oldest!" she said pridefully. "Don't think the others don't resent it!"

He could smell her nearness, the musky aroma of her body. Did her politics matter? She had duped him. On the other hand, she may have done him a favor.

"Damn the Polisario! Come her, you little traitor! I can't see your face." He strained at the cord that tied his wrists, seeking her lips.

"In the name of Allah! You are crazy. They'll kill me!" she whispered hoarsely.

"The others have eaten and they're sleeping it off. We won't move until nightfall, right?" *To hell with them*, he thought.

"Right. But don't jeopardize your chance of leaving here alive. Mine, too!" She slipped away from him and left the hut.

Marc sighed, lay back on the floor and succumbed to the heat and fatigue.

Later he awoke, aware of the rough ground and the meanness of the hovel. A strange nightmare resonated through his head. He chuckled aloud at his lack of caution; she was right of course. But one thing he knew: Aysha was drawn to him. Somehow he was special to her, which meant that no matter what happened, he was not alone in all this. But what exactly was Aysha's game? She was idealistic, of course, goaded by her past, motivated to break the fetters of Islam that women had borne for centuries. But she had moved ahead too fast, seeing it all in simplistic terms. She believed in the promise of a better life for the oppressed, but she failed to understand the barbaric cruelty of dictatorship, the form of government that prevailed in most Islamic countries.

One of the Sahraoui guards brought him to his senses with a swift kick in the thigh. Marc stood up shakily. He was groggy. His body felt grimy with dirt and sweat. *It must be dark*, he thought as he was pushed, bound and still blindfolded, into the back seat of the Renault sedan that he had rented. The two Sahraoui climbed in on either side of him. Nobody spoke, but he could hear Aysha's whisper from the front seat between the two Reguibat. Silently they drove away from Ifrane, bouncing over the uneven track. He was grateful to find himself tightly wedged between the two guards, despite their boorish hostility. Then they were on smooth pavement again. *It's the main road*, he thought, *built on the old caravan route to Senegal which I intended to follow one day. But not like this!*

He consoled himself with the thought that Lawrence had been a prisoner too. In this region many European explorers had perished at the hands of ruthless desert bands. The French missionary Charles Foucault, the luckless Camille Douls! With a spine-tingling shiver, he realized he would be lucky himself if he reached the Polisario camp. They had to cross a border swarming with Moroccan troops, whose orders undoubtedly were to shoot anything moving either way.

Marc calculated that the Renault had traveled some seventy-five miles on the paved road when the younger Reguibi, who was driving, called out Foum el Hassan. Marc smiled involuntarily. This was where he had planned, on a more leisurely trip, to have a look at prehistoric carvings of elephants and rhinos.

He felt the car swerve off the road. Now it was jolting over a dirt track once more. Abruptly the vehicle came to a halt.

"Our Land Rover is here," the driver snapped. "Keep quiet. Hurry!

"We will not be in the Sahara until we pass through the Ouarkziz mountains," he added for Marc's benefit.

The cloth was jerked from Marc's head. His wrists still bound, he stepped awkwardly from the car, blinking. He was barely able to make out the pre-Saharan scrubland in the dim moonlight. The two guards were removing a thick camouflage of twigs and branches that hid the other vehicle. Aysha's musky fragrance pervaded his senses as she moved beside him.

"We're using a Moroccan Land Rover to cross the border," she whispered. "They stole it last week. Watch out! You mean nothing to these men. Believe me, they'll slit your throat if you get in the way."

This time he knew that she was speaking the truth. With a sinking feeling he wished that she weren't with them, for her presence would complicate things if they were caught. In fact, her status vis-à-vis her own country was precarious. Moroccans were famous for taking no prisoners.

The older Reguibi was speaking to him now. "We have removed your blindfold to avoid looking suspicious. Our route should eliminate encounters, but I have to warn you..."

The younger man cut him off. "We're armed. If you cry out or make a move, you'll be shot. We are not afraid of killing an *American!*" The last word rang with sarcasm.

American journalist, target of terrorism. *We make news as well as write it,* Marc thought. But if they wanted to keep it quiet, the Polisario would have little trouble covering up his disappearance. Next to him, he felt a tremor. Was Aysha afraid for him or for herself.

The older man pointed to his companion. "He is Said, our driver. I am Rachid. The two guards are Mokhtar, with the scar, and Baba, the tall one. I warn you not to annoy either of them. The track across the desert is poor, but we know it well. We plan to reach the Polisario camp tomorrow."

"*Inchallah*, if it is God's will," Said murmured. "*Allons!* There's no time to lose!" he hissed at Marc.

He motioned him to a seat in the rear which ran along the side parallel to one on the other side. Behind him, a bulging eye leered suspiciously. The livid scar of Mokhtar's cheek danced to a series of imprecations as the stocky Sahraoui moved next to Marc. The lean, uncommunicative Baba and Rachid, the most dignified member of the group, sat facing them. The feisty Said was at the wheel. Aysha was given the passenger seat. Marc was now convinced that Rachid and Said, the fluent French speakers, were Algerians serving with the Polisario. The other two were authentic Sahraoui from the ex-Spanish Sahara. It didn't matter what they were. They'd been brought along because they knew the terrain and because they were trained to kill. You couldn't ask for a better cast of characters. His fingers itched to start writing.

"Our freedom-fighters have driven these tracks many times at night. They navigate by the stars and they have the ears of the desert fox," Rachid said. Marc believed him.

Its headlights extinguished, the Land Rover ground noisily through a set of tired gears. The track seemed hacked out of sharp-edged shale. Occasionally, Said swung the wheel sharply to miss a boulder looming ghostlike over the flatland. With his bound hands Marc steadied himself against the back of the seat.

His thoughts were far away when he heard the first shots hit the windshield. Fragments of glass were suddenly flying about the car's interior. A hail of bullets pummeled its body, and a piercing scream came from Aysha. As the vehicle careened to the right, the four bodies in the rear hurtled against one another. Across from Marc, Baba moaned. A bright beam of light to the left of them was sweeping the area, and Marc saw blood pouring from Baba's head as he fell to the floor.

"Down, all of you! Get us out of here!" Rachid shrieked at Said.

"Shut up! I know the area better than they do," Said barked, driving straight through the brush. Aysha cried out again in pain.

"Drive, idiot. We've got people hit! Moroccan sons-of-whores!" Rachid pulled a dusty cloth from his pocket which he held against Baba's head as best he could while the Land Rover crashed through a thicket.

"There's another track here!" Said's voice choked. Shaking glass fragments from his arms, he pressed on the accelerator.

"For the love of Allah, help me!" Aysha moaned in anguish.

Bouncing helplessly on the worn seat, Marc shouted to Said to stop. The wounded needed attention. His only answer was a string of Arab curses. Interminably they continued, ascending for a time, it seemed. The engine roared in low gear, fighting for every meter over loose stone. Aysha was strangely quiet.

Oh, God! She can't be dead. If only I could get to her, help her, Marc raged helplessly.

Now the moon was obscured. They were passing beneath an overhanging cliff along a stony arroyo. The dry river bed was studded with rocks, but they were moving freely. More important, they were not being pursued.

"Said, stop the car!" Marc thundered over the din. "Aysha and Baba are wounded. I've had medical training." It was a lie, but first-aid was better than nothing. He repeated himself in French and Arabic. "Are you crazy? Do you want them to bleed to death?" he shouted. Said barked an obscenity, jerking the Land Rover to a stop by a straggly bush, which provided little cover.

"We are safe for a time," Rachid said, stepping out of the vehicle. "We have crossed the pass through the Ouarkziz Mountains. Let the American loose."

Impatiently, Marc extended his arms behind him and, with one clean thrust, Mokhtar's knife blade slashed the thong. He jerked the car door open and grasped Aysha before she fell. Gently he carried her unconscious body to open ground and laid her flat.

"For God's sake, a light!" he shouted. "Have you no equipment?"

"Why bother with the bitch?" Said muttered. "Her specialty is foreigners!"

Marc swore under his breath. Had they seen him with Aysha or did they merely assume that a man and a woman had only one thing in common. *Oh, God, let her be all right!*

Rachid approached behind a wobbly circle of light. He held out the flickering flashlight.

"Hold it so I can see!" Marc scowled, scrutinizing Aysha's arm where a bullet had passed through the flesh. He washed the bleeding wound, wantonly splashing valuable drinking water from the plastic bottle Rachid held in his left hand. Darting back to the Land Rover, he seized his suitcase, threw it open and took out his one clean shirt and the first-aid kit that he had included at the last minute. With vicious haste he tore the shirt into strips and then, with slow deliberation, wound a tourniquet around her arm above the still-bleeding wound. By the shaky beam of Rachid's light, he identified a tube of antibiotic ointment and spread a thick layer on the wound. Then he laid several pieces of fresh cloth on top and tied them down firmly. He hoped the makeshift compression bandage had stopped the flow of blood, remembering that he had almost left the kit behind.

He slapped Aysha's cheek. When her eyes fluttered open, he

poured a slug of whiskey between her lips.

"Courage!" he whispered.

He felt the grateful pressure of a finger.

"Forget the whore!" Said shouted. "Baba is also hit."

Marc turned to the tall Sahraoui lying on the other side of him. He removed Rachid's sopping rag. Blood was still pouring from the temple which had been grazed by a passing bullet. Baba's clothing was soaked. The wound was not serious, Marc decided, staunching the flow with what remained of the white shirt. The man was vigorous and healthy, if uncommunicative. He didn't even cry out. *Desert stoicism*, thought Marc. *They're a strange lot.* Fortunately, he hadn't anything more serious to deal with. Now they needed professional help.

"They can't cross the desert like this!" he snapped at Rachid's lean, hovering form.

"*Merde alors*! They'll have to! A patrol will be after us. We'll have daylight in two hours and I want to be over the border!"

It was a command. Rachid turned back to the Land Rover.

"Aysha Kandicha!" Said spat malevolently, adding a foul curse. "I told you we shouldn't have brought her."

Marc had removed the tourniquet and was fixing a splint on Aysha's arm. She groaned slightly as he slipped two pills into her mouth.

"What is he saying?" he asked softly.

"Aysha Kandicha is a legend—the wife of the devil, a seductress who causes men's downfall." She coughed in pain. "No more whiskey, please."

"Aysha Kandicha!" Marc whistled softly. "You live up to your name. But you're the one who's been hit!" Above her blood-soaked shirt, he pressed a stealthy kiss on her forehead. He hoped she wouldn't pass out again. There was so little he could do for her.

"Allah's revenge for getting you into this!" she said softly.

With difficulty, Marc persuaded Rachid to allow him to sit in the front seat so that he could brace Aysha's arm. He had one thought now—to get her to a medical station.

"How much farther do we have to drive?" He realized at once that his question was stupid.

Rachid didn't bother to answer. His expression was grim. He slid behind the wheel, motioning the disgruntled Said to the rear.

An hour later in the gathering light of dawn, the lines of tension seemed to fade from Rachid's face. Now that they were beyond the border area patrolled by the Moroccan military, he became almost sociable.

Driving in the desert was easy he said, despite the risk of being mired in the sand. There were tracks to follow, hardened by the spring rains. The patchy areas of stones could be avoided in the daylight. They would pass over a few small hills before climbing the wall of the plateau, the Hammada of Tindouf. Then the ground would be rough again.

Marc pressed his ear to Aysha's mouth. She was breathing lightly, dozing.

Before them the skyline was dark and far. Above it, a veil of purple was gradually dissolving to mother-of-pearl, like the lid of an oyster slowly opening. Farther to the east, along the desert rim, fingers of pink began to bleed red. An expanse of sand and rock undulated to meet the light, a rippling brown-to-bronze sea, turning gold. In his teens, Marc had painted with watercolors, and now he found incredible beauty in the changing pastels of the desert. One day he would return and attempt to record the abstract irreality of such vistas.

Here and there the wind-twisted trunk of an acacia lifted its dusty green canopy. An occasional copse of tamarisk drifted up with sand spiraled along the desert floor. And far off, on the horizon, Marc discerned a thick slice of burnt umber creeping into view. So that was the great mesa or *hammada*, as Rachid called it, stretching off into Algeria. Somewhere on that rough table top the Polisario had their camp.

Rachid's black turban was as coated with gray powder as the beard below it. The whites of his eyeballs were a network of crimson, but his grip on the wheel was firm. Marc encouraged him to talk.

He was making a wide arc around the Tower of Merkala, he said.

There was no point in taking a risk. The Moroccans had manned the outpost for a time, though they had now abandoned most sites in the desert. For them Polisario strikes had been costly, and today the rebels moved about the desert unhampered.

"The Sahraoui know how to survive in the wilderness. The Moroccans are afraid of it. They will die here by the thousands." Rachid's words hung in the morning air like a bad omen.

In the glow of dawn Marc studied Aysha's fine-boned face. In sleep her features seemed softened and childlike. The mane of hair spread over the bloodied shirt had turned ash blond with desert dust. How young and helpless she seemed among this desert riff-raff!

Chapter Seven

High in the sky hung a lowering curtain of black as the Land Rover approached the *hammada*'s pouting overhang. A barely visible set of tracks leading to the high plateau was intermittently broken by wind-formed crescents of sand, around which Rachid charted a zigzag course. From Mokhtar and Baba came cries of anguish.

"*Irifi*," a hollow voice suddenly cried out from the rear. It was Said.

Marc glanced back from the front seat where he braced the sleeping Aysha against the door. A chalky pink balloon appeared to be rising through the black cloud that now obscured the sky. It was swelling rapidly, bearing down upon them menacingly, as though it would carry them off somewhere into the atmosphere.

"Allah, help us! A sandstorm!" muttered Rachid, clutching the wheel as the wind hit the car. "Close the windows!" he shouted.

Marc obeyed mechanically, brusquely pushing Aysha aside. Was there nothing else to be done? Were they merely helpless victims of one of nature's blind rages, he asked himself as though he might somehow stave off disaster during the brief seconds before they were engulfed.

With incandescent speed, a turbid shroud, now milky ochre in color, blotted out the afternoon sun and enveloped the Land Rover like thick soup slopped out of the sky. They were in the midst of it now. Bombarded by sand particles, the vehicle trembled, briefly defying the onslaught, then coughed and chugged to a convulsive stop. Inside, the heat was stifling, the air thick with flying sand. The six choking occupants groped for handkerchiefs, an end of turban, anything to cover mouth and nostrils.

A sirocco, the terrifying storm of the African desert, could be perilous, Marc knew. It could rage on for a week, changing the contour of the terrain, smothering every object living or dead in mausoleums of sand. He offered a tattered shirt remnant to Aysha. She seized it to cover her mouth, her chest heaving to the rhythm of deep, dry coughs. He dared do no more.

For the second time since he had been in Morocco, Marc's lips moved in prayer. They could be buried alive in a mass grave under a mountain of sand. His disappearance would be unknown and unexplained, for the Sahara wasn't on his agenda. The war zone was officially out-of-bounds for Americans. Even if they survived the sandstorm, he had no idea of what his reception would be among the lawless guerillas. In this part of the world, newsmen were considered tantamount to spies. He could be shot, or more likely, held interminably as a hostage. He remembered Aysha's tale. Justice was blind in the desert.

A sharp cry from behind jolted him. A layer of chalky powder concealed the livid scar that was Mokhtar's trademark and gave him a sepulchral pallor. He pointed a stubby finger at Marc, screeching, "*Inglizi! Djeen! Lanat Allah alik!*" The curse labeled Marc an intruding evil spirit, responsible for the attack by desert demons.

Baba burst into a loud wail, protecting his bandaged head with his hands. Swaying from side to side, he alternately moaned and chanted "*Allah in'al sitan!*" Allah should damn the devil! The hypnotic pelting of the car body, Mokhtar's ringing curse and Baba's incessant chant resounded through the murky pea soup.

Then it was over as suddenly as it had begun. Abruptly, the swirling vortex moved away from them and appeared ahead as a wall of pale ochre sucking up the desert on its way. The storm had lasted for perhaps an hour, perhaps less. It was followed by an eerie silence. Aysha was near exhaustion, her body racked with torturous coughing. Marc struggled to open the door against the mound of sand that had sifted up around the vehicle. Its other occupants were shaking layers of loose white powder from their faces and clothing, confusedly grateful like the survivors of a shipwreck. From under a back seat Mokhtar produced two shovels. Said took one, pushed open a door and began working through the sand drifts which covered the wheels.

Marc said another prayer for the motor. That was their primary concern. He busied himself clearing the hood, but kept a wary eye on Mokhtar, who was grumbling ominously to Said. The scar on his cheek was visible again, raw and ugly in the fading sunlight. Then Marc saw it coming: Mokhtar's shovel flying through the air, aimed at his head. Marc fell on the sand in the nick of time. The shovel clanked noisily off the hood, and the fierce little Sahraoui leapt at him like a crazed dog, his hands grasping for Marc's throat. Marc barely had time to flex his knee. The karate kick missed its mark, but Mokhtar's body toppled over helplessly beside him.

Marc cracked an eye to see the tall figure of Rachid looming above them. The fury in his eye, his beard bleached white with sand gave him momentarily all the majesty of Moses on the Mount. Marc stared, unbelieving. He had not suspected that the older Reguibi possessed such strength and agility. The Reguibat were the "Sons of the Clouds," "Masters of the Desert." Don't trust them, the Ma el Ainin had said. Marc thanked God for Rachid's humanity. One of them was a civilized and just individual. As he sat up, a firm hand thrust his head downward.

Said, crouching over him, confronted Rachid and spat out a torrent of words. To hell with the American! He was useless to them. El-Ouali wouldn't want him in the camp, snooping about. A damn spy! Why should they waste precious provisions on him? Meanwhile, Mokhtar had retrieved his shovel and was uttering imprecations. They were doomed by the curse he had put on the American. Do away with him! That much Marc could decipher.

Behind, Baba moaned in agony. Let them get moving again. He was in pain. Aysha stared in horror from the Land Rover, keeping out of it. She knew better than to involve herself now. Vultures they were, Marc felt, crowding around, hanging over him, bickering and squabbling before they picked his bones clean.

Rachid, speaking calmly, attempted reason. It would not be wise to harm a foreigner, especially an American. They would be hunted down like outlaws. The Polisario would be blamed. There was no profit for them in it. Mokhtar lurked malevolently behind him. If he slammed the shovel against Rachid's gray head, they were all finished, thought Marc. Damn their brutish density! While they argued with each other, the available light would be gone.

"Stop!" he shouted, cutting in. "Do you think anyone can leave? Try the motor!"

Mokhtar's dark eyes burned with frustration. Rachid nodded in agreement. Said leapt into the car seat and turned the key. There was no response. They were like children, placing implicit trust in the Western machine and having no conception of its fallibility, thought Marc.

He opened the hood, ignoring Mokhtar. Sand had silted up around the motor. The carburetor was covered. They had about one hour more of light. If he could play doctor to save his skin, he could also be a mechanic. But he had to work fast, first to get rid of the sand, then to clean the filter, blow out the gas line and try the motor again.

"Let him be!" Rachid barked. He could call up impressive reserves of authority when he wanted to. The others listened sullenly. "Get to work with the shovels and keep your noisy mouths shut!"

Marc seized a tin cup, offered by Aysha, to bail out the sand, and with the shirt remnant dusted away as much as he could. It was a slow and delicate job. He offered up another prayer. That was three times more appeals to the Almighty than he'd made in his adult life. He climbed into the front seat next to Aysha. She gave him an encouraging smile, but he could see that she was in pain. She was hollow-eyed and pale, but her mouth was set in a determined line. How long could she last? Again and again he turned the key, pressed the accelerator. Again and again the result was a rumble, a sputter, a cough-out. Said howled with glee. "*Inglizi!*" had failed.

Marc turned to Rachid. "It's useless anyway. We've no gas. We've used up the jerry cans!"

Rachid smiled and motioned him to keep trying. He would soon learn the secret of Polisario success. The face of the desert was riddled with caches of supplies—gas, munitions, food. They hadn't far to go. With those heartening words, Marc succeeded. A cheerful belch erupted from the motor and it began to rumble steadily.

The sun had set when Rachid moved into the driver's seat and started off again over the now- trackless desert. *It's hopeless*, thought Marc. There wasn't anything out there. Nothing could be stored under the shifting sands and found after that storm. They were heading for a crevasse at the base of the *hammada*, where deep erosions in the red brown façade gave a curious fluting effect. Rachid stopped the Land Rover near the crevasse, and Mokhtar and Said jumped out with shovels and commenced to dig into the side of the meseta. Watching them, Marc wondered what mysterious marking told them where to look. Eventually, a wall of orange clay collapsed, leaving a yawning hole.

Said, shrieking with glee, almost tripped over his unraveling turban as he charged into the cave. Marc helped Aysha, and Baba stumbled after them. Within the cool interior, Said was ripping ravenously into boxes of supplies, bottled water, cans of meat, sardines and fruit, and powdered milk. Marc found a box of medical supplies, cloths that looked reasonably clean, and ointments. He changed Aysha's and Baba's dressings while the others tore savagely into the food.

Rachid had had the presence of mind to start a fire. They were now well into Algerian territory beyond the reach of Moroccan patrols, he said with patrician authority. But they had over a hundred kilometers of rough terrain to cover on top of the *hammada*. They should sleep while they could. No one had the temerity or the desire to refute him.

Somewhat refreshed, Aysha had regained her color. She sat across from Marc, looking into the fire with the inscrutable smile of the Sphinx. She seemed deeply absorbed in her thoughts. She couldn't, or wouldn't, talk to him with the others there. He wondered about her status among them. It permitted her to travel with them, yet they kept their distance from her. Young Said's bitter resentment of her was apparent. Rachid was politely correct with her. It didn't seem possible that they would treat other women in this manner. The Arab female could be tough, he thought. Forced into loveless marriages, harems even, until very recently, they harbored few illusions. They snatched happiness where they could. But Aysha was fashioned by changing times. Partially educated in the West and liberated from Muslim strictures, she had chosen to throw her cards in with the Polisario. He sensed that she enjoyed playing with danger.

Marc shivered. A night alone in the cave was a cold, miserable prospect, especially after the searing heat of the day. The others, even Aysha, seemed inured to it. They rolled themselves into great balls of black wool around the dying fire. The blanket he had been given reeked of sheep oil and felt leaden rather than warm. He gazed into the embers with one obsessive thought: *Another log!* But wood was the scarcest, most precious commodity in the desert, after water. He dared not. Mokhtar would spring on him like a desert lynx. Then he wondered how many outsiders had seen a Polisario cache, never mind sleeping in one. He felt annoyed that he was missing another on-the-spot story! Why hadn't somebody invented a portable telex? He would have liked to bowl over the Sahraoui with a display of low-tech wizardry. But that would surely have cooked his goose!

The next morning Aysha claimed that she could sit by herself in the passenger seat. Her wound, now bandaged, was giving her less discomfort. She had slept long and hard after taking Marc's painkillers. She seemed pensive, and so Marc left her alone. He had done what he could for her.

As for himself, every muscle ached after a night of tossing on the rocklike floor of the damp cave. He would never qualify as a "Son of the Clouds," he thought grimly. He attempted a few limp push-ups and joined the others in the back of the Land Rover. Mokhtar sulked, while Said took over at the wheel. Marc was glad that Rachid was sitting across from him.

A narrow track wound up the side of the *hammada*, and they were soon hammering over stony terrain toward Tindouf. Once a great slave market and crossing point of caravan routes, the town was historically a focal point for Reguibat tribes, he recalled from his research. They had, at one time, paid taxes to the Sultan, and Morocco's claim to the Western Sahara was based on that fact. French troops had "pacified" the Reguibat in 1934, which meant of course that they had beaten them into submission. But still there was no official border laid out between Algeria and Morocco, and the area remained a sort of no man's land. Skirmishes broke out after both countries achieved independence, Morocco in 1956 and Algeria in 1962, and the region reeked of bad blood long before the Polisario came into existence.

Rachid wedged a pile of clothing under him to cushion his lean buttocks. Over his gray-white beard he looked skeptically at Marc, who had a feeling that he didn't measure up to Reguibat standards. His complexion was pallid rather than bronze, his straight hair sandy-colored and unkempt rather than black and neatly curled to the scalp. He was lame and sore from sleeping on the ground.

"Westerners do not understand the desert," Rachid observed drily. "They battle against nature, try to dominate it and eventually exploit and spoil it. On the other hand, the Bedouin live in harmony with their environment. They have no needs beyond what they find at hand." For the Sahraoui, it was possible to exist quite happily without all that the West holds dear—without cities, industries, roads and automobiles, even without money. Barter was the preferred form of exchange. The women especially chose living in tents in the open desert over city life. In the desert, a woman was as free as a man to come and go. In town, she had to stay at home and wear a veil if she ventured forth to go shopping. The government had experimented with giving them housing. The women moved in at first and then they changed their minds and moved out again. The two men laughed and then lapsed into silence. Talking was difficult while the car lurched over rocks and stones.

For all his know-how with medicine and motors, Marc felt he wasn't much of a candidate for desert life. On the horizon he welcomed the sight of a tent here and there. With rising expectations, he realized that they were approaching the headquarters of the Polisario Front, not far from the ancient town of Tindouf.

Chapter Eight

At first sight, the Bedouin encampment appeared hardly menacing. Strings of tents, some gray-white, some black, scattered over the wind-swept sand, looked strangely desolate. Perhaps there were two hundred tents in the Polisario camp, plus a few prefabricated structures, flimsy intruders not destined to survive. In the oppressive heat of the afternoon, nothing stirred. No bird flew across the desolate plateau. As far as the eye could see, only the fluttery wave of a mirage danced along the horizon.

The Land Rover stopped by a strange moonscape of junk, a cemetery of rusting, haphazardly strewn carapaces. Fenderless, motorless, tireless vehicles littered the sand like cast-off toys. Rachid pointed with pride. Captured Moroccan armored cars and personnel carriers had been hauled many kilometers over the desert to the camp. Their parts were useful.

Said and Mokhtar leapt enthusiastically from the Land Rover to inspect a new arrival, which Marc recognized as the half-demolished wreck of a U.S.-made medium tank. Above it, a gun barrel sagged like the beak of a brooding bird and, above that, the new republic's standard, bearing an Islamic crescent and star, hung limply in the lifeless air.

Aysha was already out of the car. With a wave of her functioning arm, she disappeared in the direction of one of the pre-fabs, where the clinic was apparently situated. She would see Marc later on, she had said. He had no idea what was in store for him. She had revealed nothing. Perhaps she didn't know. Aysha had become as noncommittal as the Sphinx of Giza. She was one of them again. Damn her! He had counted on her help at the camp. Now he wondered grimly whether he would ever see her again.

Later, within the tent to which he was assigned, Marc spread his aching limbs on the only furniture provided, a rough mattress of straw. His feet extended foolishly a foot over the end of it and he could feel the sharp ends of straw through the two leaden blankets supplied him. Like all desert people, the Polisario functioned mainly in the cool of the night, and he was glad they had given him a tent to himself to rest until late afternoon.

Peering under the tent flap, he had spied his guard, skulking to one side, his Kalashnikov assault rifle hanging on the ready. It reminded him of an old engraving that he had seen in Tangier, depicting traditional Berber hospitality. Charging horsemen in medieval regalia were dispatched to welcome the stranger—and lure him into captivity. Many Westerners who wandered into Morocco had found that captivity could be quite luxurious. As if to verify his thought, a boy slipped into the tent with a steaming glass of mint tea and a flat round of bread. From under heavy lashes the child stole shy glances at the tall American, then scampered off as though the devil were pitchforking his heels. It was a good sign, thought Marc. Bedouin curiosity might serve him well.

After sundown, a young man in well-worn khaki fatigues opened the flap and beckoned brusquely with his rifle. Following his silent escort, Marc saw that the camp had now become a beehive of activity. The atmosphere was festive. Tent flaps were up, women and older men milled about, chatting and talking. Clusters of bronze faces shone in the yellow glare of burning braziers. His nose detected the familiar sweet-smoky aroma of burning charcoal and singed meat dipped in cumin, and his insides ached with hunger for real food. But his eyes were drinking it all in. The camp itself was a treasure trove of local color. Somewhere, a radio droned Arab music.

A voice boomed unexpectedly. "No peace until total independence—Radio Free Sahara." Marc's escort beamed at Marc, shaking his fist. The American strove to make out the rush of Arabic that followed: redistribution of property, eradication of exploitation, organization of collectives. *Hefty words*, he thought. They were going to turn the damn desert into the Leninist equivalent of the Garden of Eden!

A piercing shriek cut into the radio transmission.

"King Hassan, the Western stooge is dead! The Moroccan imperialist invader killed by his own people!" a voice shrilled from nearby. Marc spun around. Hassan II dead? He poked his head inside the nearest tent, where a bizarre performance was taking place.

A colorfully robed figure fell flat. Several times it righted itself, then fell again, bashed on the head by a Bedouin. Screams of laughter mingled with a crescendo of shrieks. Ould Daddah, the President of Mauritania, tried to help. To no avail. King Hassan had been finished off! Shouts of glee. Then suddenly the puppet show was over.

The audience was entirely female. Swathed in black shawls that bound their heads to their bodies in one shapeless mass, the women rocked on their haunches, clapping and hurling strange ululations from the backs of their throats. Amid the brouhaha, a few nursed infants, batting occasionally at clumps of flies glued to the babies' eyes. A massive woman rose. From within the folds of her opaque robes she produced a dusty palm to shake Marc's. The other women howled with laughter. He was the sideshow now, this alien with sickly white skin!

He felt a sharp prod and hastily backed out of the tent, as his taciturn escort motioned him on.

The next tent was wide open. Here a group of old men were cutting leather for sandals. Marc tried a salutation in Spanish, and a weather-ravaged face brightened.

"*Sí, sí, muy buenos días!*" The old man smiled toothlessly.

Here then was a man from the Spanish Sahara. Behind him a group of small boys in tattered remnants of clothing were chanting an unrecognizable singsong. Marc couldn't help but note an opaque eyeball here, a slit eye there, the persistent flies sucking at corners of mouths. Poor little beggars, they were learning Spanish, it seemed. Staring down on this activity were two giant poster-photographs—a heavily bearded Fidel Castro and the lean face of Muammar Qadhafi peering from under an outsized officer's cap. Marc's guide pointed his rifle pridefully at these deities, and they moved on to a large black-and-white striped tent.

At its opening a darkly handsome young man in a clean khaki uniform extended his hand and announced himself in impeccable French as "Bashir Mustapha Sayed, Deputy Secretary General of the S.A.D.R." A dimple fluttered in Bashir's right cheek as he explained that a month ago the founding of the Saharan Arab Democratic Republic had been celebrated in this very tent. Marc murmured regret at having missed the occasion and followed him inside where several uniformed men were gathered. Bashir didn't seem like a bad type. So far so good. Marc decided to keep his eyes open and save his complaints for the Polisario chief.

Aligned like birds on a telephone wire, a row of older men in indigo robes and black turbans nodded from a bench in the center and continued cackling among themselves. These were Sahraoui tribal chiefs, Bashir said, and introduced Marc as the American Ambassador to Morocco. Marc didn't bother to correct him. Their goggle-eyes indicated he might as well have come from the moon.

One old fellow, introduced as "Chibani," fixed Marc with a riveting glare as he blurted a string of words. After a few repetitions, Marc understood, "The wind from Morocco can never reach us!"

Marc shook his hand heartily, and Old Chibani laughed until his eyes watered and the spittle ran down his white beard. Behind him, the younger men strained to get a look at the American.

With an impatient gesture, Bashir motioned to Marc to be seated and proceeded to launch into a harangue extolling the short history of the Saharan Arab Democratic Republic. The unarmed Sahraouis had fled the invasion of the Western Sahara by the Moroccan army. Now their Algerian brothers had given them shelter. They were fighting for their right to exist as an independent republic.

Here a craggy-faced officer broke in, announcing himself as Ould Seheir, Commander of the Northern Front. The Polisario would bring down the government of both Mauritania and Morocco if their troops didn't get out of the Sahara. Mauritania was unstable. As for Morocco, kings had gone out of style! This brought down the house. Much shoulder-slapping followed, and old Chibani and his colleagues broke into loud guffaws.

Marc's eyes lighted up as they followed his nose to a steaming tray that had just entered the tent. For three days he had not had a real meal. Now, seated on the ground along with the others, he tore as they did into the gristly meat with his bare hands. Perhaps it was camel, perhaps goat. He didn't care. It was hot and it tasted good.

Still eating, Marc turned to the guerilla commander. How did his men survive in the desert? he asked

"*Très bien!*" Ould Seheir's doughty grimace indicated that he had few laggards. "The guerillas are tough. They go out for days at a time. Often they find their own food. Outsiders think the desert is flat. But, no, there are mountains, ravines, river beds, plenty of cover for Jeeps if one knows the terrain. The Polisario pounce on Moroccan troops in isolated outposts. They wipe them out or put them on the run."

Ould Seheir's sun-blistered lips closed momentarily on a chunk of meat, then he continued speaking. The Moroccans had another serious problem. In 1971, after the attempts on his life, the King had given the order that a number of his generals be shot, and they hadn't been replaced. The leadership of the Royal Armed Forces was severely impaired. Now every order, every permission to use firearms, had to come directly from the King. When those poor goons saw the enemy coming, they couldn't open fire until they received the order from Rabat—which, due to poor communications, frequently didn't come. Sure, sure, the Moroccans acquitted themselves well in World War II and on Syria's Golan Heights. The Moroccan was a great soldier in conventional warfare. In the desert he was lost. Ould Seheir's strident laugh was cut short.

A sudden stirring of whispers rippled through the crowd. The military sprang to their feet. A slight young man in khaki had appeared at the tent flap. The elderly Sahraoui stared, then shuffled sullenly out of the tent. Bashir introduced El-Ouali Mustapha Sayed,

Secretary-General of the Saharan Republic, who was followed by his ministers of foreign affairs, security and defense. *My God*, thought Marc, *they're kids. They're all in their twenties! Where did they come from?*

E-Ouali's black brows formed a straight line under the dark curls of a full afro. The heavy lips were tightly pursed between a thick black mustache and a trim goatee. His fleshless cheeks were concave under high cheekbones. The man seemed taut as a live wire. For a moment Marc felt himself seared by obsidian eyes. Then the Sahraoui leader sat down.

When El-Ouali spoke, it was in fluent, educated French. It was a pleasure to host the first American at the camp, he said. The words were courteous, but the black eyes scrutinized the American with open hostility. Marc felt oddly ill at ease, sensing that, for some reason, the Polisario leader detested him personally. The spoken word of an Arab rarely matched his thoughts, for in Marc's experience word was rhetoric; only body language had meaning. No matter what El-Ouali said, his eyes spoke the truth. Marc's gut feeling was that he had to take a stand now or be taken for a fool. He wanted his news story, and he wanted to get it out soon.

And so he opened with a broadside in French, in which he was more fluent than in Arabic. "I demand to know why I, an American citizen, a foreign correspondent in no way involved in desert politics, have been taken captive. I demand to know why I have been brought by force to this camp and held as a prisoner. The action flouts every recognized international convention."

"*Mais non!*" El-Ouali's lips seemed cast in a sardonic smile. "In the eyes of the SADR, Mr. Lamont, you are a distinguished guest. We hope that you are being so treated in the camp."

Marc cut in. "The insult to my country can't be lightly dismissed! In fact, it will substantially lessen public support for the Polisario cause." That was a joke! How many Americans had even heard of the Western Sahara?

The guerilla leader smiled. Personally, he regretted any inconvenience to his visitor caused by his overzealous men.

Furthermore, the SADR's ally and benefactor, Algeria, had many friends in Washington, he explained. America's commercial interests were well served by its ties with Algeria. The SADR would also like to consider America its friend.

El-Ouali had him there, Marc thought. Algeria possessed large resources of both oil and natural gas; that figured importantly in the energy crisis following OPEC's raising of the price of oil two years ago.

El-Ouali continued, cunningly confident. The SADR National Council hoped that after his visit Mr. Lamont would take a favorable impression of the Sahraoui republic back to the U.S.A. Three-quarters of a million Sahraoui could not be denied their right to statehood. He trusted that, as an arms supplier, America would understand the futility of backing Morocco, which offered America nothing.

"That will be decided in Washington," Marc said stiffly, not missing the grossly inflated Sahraoui population statistic. "I would like to request permission to roam freely in the camp and to speak with whomever I choose. Following that, I request safe transport to Morocco."

"Et pourquoi?" Ignoring Marc's first request, El-Ouali's battle-hardened torso leaned close to Marc. Why was Mr. Lamont in a hurry to return? The war was bleeding Morocco. The King was a clever diplomat, but no fighter. In truth, he didn't know how to command a war in the desert. Eventually, the corrupt regime would fall of its own weight. Victory for the Polisario lay in the near future or the far future. It made little difference.

Right on, thought Marc. The Polisario had time on its side, time to foment dissension in Morocco, even to plot coups against the King. The SADR had more experience in guerilla tactics than statehood. He made a mental note to probe around for signs of his nemesis, Oufkir. They had to be getting their expertise somewhere.

"You are a newsman. Stay here then and write about us," said El-Ouali more congenially.

"All right, but then I'll need to have the true story," Marc said. He posed a few questions about the people in the camps—where they came from, how they lived. Then he asked how many foreign advisors were helping out.

El-Ouali's face darkened. The question was loaded. "Why would we need advisors? We know the desert. We are strong and we are many." He turned to Bashir.

"Brother! Give the American a tour tomorrow. He has much to learn!" With this, El-Ouali turned on his heel and left the tent. He was followed by his three youthful ministers of state who had contributed nothing to the meeting. Marc wondered about their expertise and regretted not having a chance to speak with them individually. With his brashness, he himself had brought an end to the meeting.

Minutes later Bashir's tall figure preceded Marc through the camp. All was quiet. The fires were out, tent flaps closed. The Bedouin were bundled in against the frigid night air. Marc was perplexed. The Polisario leadership appeared to be a close-knit, well-educated group, limited to a handful of young men. Bashir had affirmed that El-Ouali and he were actually blood brothers. Other than that he had nothing to say. Probably El-Ouali preferred to do all the talking himself. But there were still so many unanswered questions. Particularly, why had El-Ouali seemed so hostile to him?

Feeling a hand upon his arm, Marc jumped involuntarily. He had seen nothing.

"Quiet! I'm coming to your tent. Don't make a sound." A voice, speaking in English heavy with accent—a voice that had a familiar ring. It had to be someone he knew from Morocco. A figure melted into the shadow of a tent, and Marc moved on after Bashir.

Alone within the tent, he sat down on his less-than-inviting mattress. Wondering about the voice, he studied the strange shadows cast by the oil lamp that Bashir had lit, flickering uncertainly across the ridgepole that held the woven goathair in place.

"Put out the light!" a hoarse voice commanded.

He had just time to recognize the heavy-set figure, the gray-speckled beard, before the tent went black. It was Malki, the Syrian doctor from Marrakech, the clown with the musical combo. Marc

72

stared in disbelief.

"We meet again, Mr. Lamont. Always in the night!"

"So you do work for the Polisario!" Marc said. How easily he had been taken in by this buffoon! "I thought as much. Why the need for secrecy here?"

"No, no! Don't get it wrong. I'm with Moroccan security." Dr. Malki's voice was barely audible. For a decade, he had been supplying intelligence on various groups in Marrakech. Lately he had gained Polisario confidence and had been invited to the camp. They assumed, of course, that as a Syrian, he would work for them. The Syrians tended to support radical causes, right? But playing both sides wasn't easy. These men were dangerously capricious in their thinking.

"I've come to warn you, Marc. They are feeding you a slew of propaganda. It's important that you get the true picture before you leave."

"*Ecoutez bien!*" Dr. Malki continued. "The Polisario claim to have almost a million Sahraoui from the Spanish Sahara in camp. Actually, the number is well under a hundred thousand, but daily they're taking in refugees from all over the drought-ridden Sahel region to the south, from Mali and Niger particularly. In the United Nations and around the world, they are presenting these people as bona fide Sahraoui to create the image of a nation fighting for its freedom and to beef up their cause in Europe and the United States. The Red Cross is already helping them out."

Marc indulged in a self-satisfied smile. He knew that E-Ouali's figure was way off. The Spanish census of 1974, only two years ago, counted seventy-four thousand denizens of the Western Sahara. Was that why the kids were learning Spanish, he asked. To give the impression that all these people came from the Spanish colony? Didn't the world know that there were no natural resources in the desert to sustain such a population?

Malki nodded and hurried on as though time were too precious for speculation. The Polisario had set up a propaganda office in Algiers run by Cubans. False communiqués citing desert victories were being beamed around the world every day. But in these, the

Polisario didn't admit to its reliance on foreign advisors, of course. They were scattered about the Polisario camp sites—East German and Cuban, as well as Algerian. During Marc's visit, they would be kept out of sight. Marc would also have noticed that there were no young men around. That was because the training was done in another camp and the Polisario had no wish to see that particular activity described in the foreign press. The idea they wanted to get across was that the valiant Bedouin were doing it all on their own.

Naturally he would also be deprived of a viewing of the Soviet arms that had been piling up at the camp depot—SAM missiles, tanks, weapons of all kinds. Malki was trying to get information on this material, which it was rumored Libya was supplying and paying for. Before he left, Marc should try to get a look at it. It was because of the technologically advanced hardware, of course, that they needed advisors. They were having enough trouble teaching Bedouin to drive Jeeps, never mind how to launch missiles

Marc had heard the battle communiqués, of course, but he needed to know who the Polisario leaders actually were. Where did they come from?

"Youngsters, as you saw for yourself," Dr. Malki chuckled. "The old desert chiefs are merely for show, to keep the tribes happy. The Sayed brothers, El-Ouali and Bashir, run everything. They were born on the Algerian *hammada* somewhere along the unmarked border. A year or two ago El-Ouali was studying law at Mohamed V University in the Moroccan capital—on a Moroccan scholarship mind you—along with a few other SADR leaders. Only this handful have a real education. Among the others, several are Algerian; the foreign minister is Mauretanian. You see what I mean, there's hardly anyone from the Western Sahara involved. By the way, the one to watch out for is the renegade Moroccan Oufkir. He's simply a cold-blooded murderer."

Marc snorted. "Oufkir jumped me outside your house in Marrakech!"

"He was watching me," Malki said. "He thought you were trying to recruit me in a joint Moroccan-American security arrangement.

That's what they're most afraid of. You would have been passed off as a tourist casualty in Marrakech. I had a hard time convincing him that you're a journalist and nothing more.

"Look, Marc, in their way, the Polisario are decent chaps. They believe they have a real cause. Their methods are unsavory, but I think they're being duped and used for bigger stakes.

"My advice to you is, above all, avoid being detained in the camp. Conditions are life-threatening. The refugees have brought with them their famine-induced pestilences—cholera, diptheria, and polio. At this moment half of the younger children are dying of an epidemic of measles."

They heard voices outside the tent. Malki's fingers closed on Marc's arm.

"This could finish me," he hissed.

A flashlight beamed through the tent flap, followed by Bashir's tall figure and two guerillas.

Without missing a beat, Malki's bantering voice greeted them in Arabic. "What an occasion to have the visit of a foreign journalist! I have been explaining the aims of the Polisario to the American."

Talking a steady stream, Malki left with the frowning Bashir.

Marc breathed deeply. Malki was a tightrope-walker. He knew the balancing act far better than Marc, but both of them were on thin ice in the Polisario camp.

Refugees streaming in from the Sahel. Lies and propaganda coming out of Algiers. SAM missiles! How had they gotten hold of them? He tried to figure it out, but he could no longer concentrate. He had a fleeting thought of Aysha. Then he fell into a deep sleep, too exhausted to feel the prick of his bed of nails—the straw mattress.

75

Chapter Nine

Ra'ana snapped to attention. In the morning sun, her slender body was vaguely discernible under her bulky white *gondoura*. A Kalashnikov rifle rested awkwardly on her shoulder. *Like a young pony tossing her black hair around*, thought Marc. Ra'ana was in command of the Women's Camp, responsible for the military training of girls. She seemed barely twenty herself.

"You won't see any veils here!" She eyed the American, suppressing a giggle. By now, Marc realized how ridiculous he looked to them with his light hair, his pallid skin, his pale blue eyes. He felt distinctly out of place, yet not unwelcome in this instance, at least.

Bashir, frowning at her levity, was off on one of his discourses. In colonial times girls were sold into marriage by age twelve or thirteen. The Polisario was changing all that. Now women carried responsibility and fulfilled duties important to the community. This group was learning to run the camps to free men for the fighting.

"We can defend ourselves, too!" Ra'ana interrupted gaily. "Soon we shall go along with the mobile assault parties."

Bashir's ironic smile indicated that the liberation of women hadn't progressed that far.

The younger they were the more readily they swallowed the whole thing, Marc thought. It was convenient for the Polisario to use the women. They needed every bit of manpower they could get their hands on. It was a neat trick to blame traditional Berber marriage customs on the French!

"In Algeria, women died fighting for their nation's independence fourteen years ago," he said. "Now they have been forced to retreat behind their veils—in a male-dominated society. Is that going to happen in the Sahara?" Bashir gave a dour translation into Arabic.

"Never!" Ra'ana shrieked, thumping her Soviet rifle on the sandy ground.

A desert flower, Marc thought. *An untutored Aysha.* His heart ached. What had happened to Aysha? He hadn't seen her since they had arrived in the camp. He had received nothing but evasive answers to his questions from Bashir, his ever-present guide. Somehow he had to find her.

Bashir nodded coldly toward the Jeep. His current aloofness probably stemmed from Malki's stealthy visit to Marc's tent the night before. But Bashir had proven to be a fountain of information. The only drawback was that every iota of it would have to be verified.

When Marc asked about how the population had been divided up in the camp, Bashir responded as always with a barrage of data. There were three camps. The Sahraoui had been divided and subdivided into small groups of mixed tribal elements. Eleven persons shared a tent and the chores that went with it. The young were educated in one camp, and the men were trained in another.

Marc made no comment. The Polisario knew what they were doing. By breaking up tribal and family ties, they were effectively eroding the fabric of desert society. The Nazis established youth camps, too. Because the famished refugees received food, lodging and medical care, they would never object.

Casually, he asked to visit the prison camp. Bashir shook his head. It was far away across the desert. They had separated the various camps as a precaution against air attack, but Marc could talk to some Moroccan officers taken in recent fighting. Bashir drove the Jeep over a patch of open sand to a shabby tent guarded by armed guerillas.

In the suffocating atmosphere within, five ill-kempt young men sat, staring listlessly at the ground between their knees. They barely lifted their eyes to take note of the visitors. Their dark green Moroccan uniforms, stripped of rank, were discolored with dirt and perspiration. They had been attached to the Third Armored Brigade at Bir Lahlou,

Bashir said. The Polisario force, a column of mobile units, had swept into the garrison town at dawn and taken it with little resistance.

Lt. Aziz Boukili riveted his hollow-eyed gaze on Marc, answering Bashir's prodding in an embarrassed monotone. His men had been demoralized by repeated Polisario raids. They were sitting targets for hit-and-run attacks. Communications with Rabat, the Moroccan capital, were poor. No one in Morocco wanted to serve in the Sahara anymore! Bashir nodded approvingly.

Sneak in, strike, run! Highly efficient, Marc thought. The Polisario were indulging in a modernized version of the centuries-old camel raid. The traditional *razzia* were more effective than ever with Land Rovers.

The gaunt, disheveled man next to the lieutenant was a captured fighter pilot named Brahim Najeb.

"What can one do about the *katibas*?" he asked dully. These groups of three or four vehicles were hard to spot from the air. They were armed with SAM missiles. If he came down to strafe, he ran the risk of being picked off by machine-gun fire—it had happened to a friend. He himself had been shot down by a missile at 6,000 feet. Fighter aircraft were useless in desert warfare. Morocco needed helicopters and reconnaissance planes.

"Why didn't you cross the Algerian border and bomb the Polisario camp?" Marc asked the pilot. Bashir threw him a searching glance.

The pilot's hand moved in a gesture of futility. His eyes blazed with hopeless fury. "We would if we could! The King holds us back. With a handful of old U.S. F-5s, we're no match for them. Algeria has hundreds of MiG-25s, 21s and the latest models!"

Marc felt a gnawing anguish for the wasted youth of these men. Their condition was degrading and humiliating now. How much worse off they would be when they joined hundreds of other prisoners in the remote camp, set off by itself in the blistering desert. There was nothing he could do for them but express the hope that the fighting would end.

Bashir eased his tall body into the driver's seat with a satisfied expression.

"By now you have learned that the Moroccans should quit the Sahara!" he said cheerily, putting the vehicle in gear.

Marc pondered the prisoners' plight. How frustrating the war must be for Moroccan pilots! Algeria's vast air superiority rendered sorties over the camps impossible, and Brahim Najeb had confirmed Dr. Malki's information. The Polisario guerillas were using state-of-the-art technology, Russian SAM missiles.

Back in the center of the camp, Bashir stopped before a slapped-together structure of prefabricated metal. "The Clinic" looked none too sturdy, but Marc's spirits soared. He'd have news of Aysha.

A uniformed guerilla pulled Bashir aside to deliver an urgent message. The moment was opportune. Slipping into the makeshift hospital, Marc found himself in a small anteroom. A woman in a thick black *gondoura* threw him a quizzical glance. Behind her, a black man in army fatigues was arranging medicines in a cabinet.

Marc's Arabic had proved largely ineffective in the desert. Testing his limited Spanish, he asked about the patient Aysha Larosien who had been shot in the arm. Could he speak to the doctor?

"*Hombre*! There is no doctor here. Only me!" The young man spun around and introduced himself as Raimondo Gonzalez, a paramedic.

A sickening quiver unsettled Marc's stomach.

"Your friend is fortunate! I was trained by the Soviets," the paramedic exclaimed.

The bullet had missed the major blood vessel. Otherwise, she might have bled to death. The humerus was fractured, but it wasn't serious. It had helped very much that she had received an antibiotic right away.

A wave of relief swept over Marc. He hoped the paramedic knew what he was talking about.

"Are there other Cubans in the camp?" Marc asked, making a guess at the man's nationality and aware that he was sticking his neck out. Fortunately, in this part of the world he passed for a European. These days the average Cuban was not very fond of Americans.

"*Seguro!*" A hundred Cuban military advisors, mostly trained in the Soviet Union, were here. They worked with a crack team of East Germans, organizing security and sending mobile units out on the desert. Their men were good with the SAM 6s and 7s. Surely, his guest had heard of their leader, the celebrated Izquierdo?

Marc blinked. Who hadn't? Izquierdo was infamous. He trained terrorists all over the world.

Having found a soul who understood Spanish, the paramedic waxed loquacious. The Cubans were helping the Sahraoui create a model socialist state in North Africa. Fidel Castro was a personal friend of Algeria's President Boumediene. It was rumored, in fact, that he was sending General Ochoa over for a visit soon.

The nurse in the black shift stared at the men, uncomprehending. Marc stared at the paramedic. It was the notorious Ochoa who organized Colonel Menghistu's bloody takeover in Ethiopia. Terrorism was child's play to him. He toppled governments! He was a big fish for this little bowl.

A rough jolt nearly knocked Marc off balance. He felt himself propelled to the door. Bashir barked sharply at the woman in black. If he understood Spanish, there would be hell to pay! Marc threw a reassuring glance at the astonished Cuban and followed Bashir to the Jeep.

Bashir didn't speak. His face was knotted with anger. Curtly he guided the American to his tent and alerted the guard.

Inured to its needles, Marc sat down thoughtfully on his mattress. For half an hour he made notes of what he had seen and heard. Obviously, he had overstepped his limits talking with the paramedic. He hoped Bashir wasn't aware that the Cuban had spilled some weighty data. As for himself, he had covered a lot of territory, but he hadn't covered it all. Plenty of questions remained—such as, where were the men? In the camp he had encountered old men, women and children. Aside from Polisario officials, there was a curious absence of young males in the camp. Would he get to see the camp where the military advisors trained the guerillas for action? Where had they stashed the Soviet military equipment? And where was it coming from? Who were their suppliers? If the Polisario sought U.S. approval, they certainly weren't opening up to the press.

Marc raised his eyes. The youngster was back, curious as ever, peering at him over a plate of muddy-looking stew. An instant later, he had torn off into the night. The meat was stringy and tough, but probably a lot more palatable than what the prisoners were getting. Marc glanced at the Algerian newspaper articles, neatly stacked for his use by a kerosene lamp. It was an improvement over the oil lamp, but its fuzzy circle of light made a difficult chore of reading. His attention strayed. He had begun to feel edgy. How would he get back to Morocco? The desolate stillness of the desert night was affecting his nerves. He felt rubbery coils constricting his abdomen.

He had begun to skim the Algerian accounts of SADR feats when in the corner of his eye he caught a movement at the opening of his tent. He leapt to his feet, his clenched fists his only defense.

A shrouded figure stepped lightly into the tent. The hood fell back and he saw Aysha slip away from the *djellaba* covering her.

"You might get shot again, invading a man's tent in the middle of the night!" he said, grinning shakily.

She came toward him cradling her left arm in its new splint. Amid the grime and dust, she exuded freshness. Her dark brown hair shone in a luxuriant coil behind her head. Her safari suit was immaculate.

"How's your arm?" Marc asked stupidly, keenly aware of his own filth and the odor he was becoming used to. He hadn't bathed in days.

He moved away to avoid contact. Picking up one of his coarse blankets, he placed it behind her as she sat stretching the shapely limbs he knew so well. He felt a dull ache in his loins; her body was so familiar.

"My first wound in action." She laughed triumphantly, ignoring his chagrin. The gold speckles in her eyes shone like pale fire. They might have been in a bar in Agadir.

"The handsome Cuban *médico* has much expertise! Soviet training is the world's best, right?" His irony fell flat. He sounded idiotically jealous.

Her eyes narrowed. She placed a cautioning finger on her lips. "I came to warn you. You're in danger!" He had asked too many questions. The Cuban had reported everything. Said was noising around that he was a spy. At the moment, the National Council was debating what to do with him. Dr. Malki had already been sent to the prison camp.

Marc swore under his breath. Malki in the disease-ridden camp! Malki had known it was coming. That was why he had taken the risk of coming to Marc's tent. He had passed on what he knew. He would pay for it, and so perhaps would Marc.

He feigned a nonchalance he didn't feel. "I haven't done a damn thing but tour the camp and listen to propaganda."

"Marc, the Polisario game *is* propaganda!" she hissed. "They don't have a foothold in the Sahara. They strike, then they run back to Algeria—that's all! Now they have to convince the outside world that they are a nation deprived of their homeland. They need a publicity campaign to obtain votes in the Organization of African Unity and the United Nations. That's why reporters like you are so important to them."

She adjusted her injured arm. Eventually this camp would be open to the foreign press as an example of thriving socialism, but they weren't ready to show it off yet. Construction lagged, medical equipment was woefully inadequate, the sanitation program was a joke. And this was the showcase camp! The Sahraoui council thought Marc had already seen too much. They had spoken of shipping him off to the prison camp with Dr. Malki before he had a chance to file a report. Marc saw the nervous flutter of black lashes. What was her game?

"Just a minute, Aysha. Whose side are you on? Is this the dedicated Polisario agent who brought me here?" Had he actually shaken her faith in the SADR?

"I work for the Polisario!" she spat out. "You could be useful. Americans should know that a progressive, anti-imperialist state has been born in the Sahara!" She paused after this burst of cant. "Besides, you were dying to get up to your neck in this adventure!" Her knowing smile reduced him to the status of a schoolboy.

"Why are you concerned about me now?" he asked, seething inside. How much of what she said could he believe?

"I'm an agent, if you like, not an assassin. I don't want to see you hurt." She was serious now.

Some members of the National Council urged that he be made a hostage, to keep the U.S. from supplying arms to Morocco. Other disagreed, but wished to hang on to him for a few months. They didn't want his reports coming out yet.

"A few months! Impossible! I refuse!" Marc snapped. He studied her, sensing an inside connection.

Aysha shook her head. He was in no position to refuse to do anything. The Polisario could be ruthless. His tent was watched day and night. In fact, she had slipped the guard a little *baksheesh* to get in.

"Money talks around here, because no one knows when, and if, they are going to be paid." She seized his hand.

"You're paid?" He cocked an eyebrow at her.

"Quite well. I have to live in Rabat. The translating is a front." Aysha's lips curved in a roguish smile.

It was evident that her status was special. He decided to lob the question that had been nagging him.

"You know one hell of a lot about what goes on in the National Council!"

Aysha withdrew her hand.

"El-Ouali is a personal friend," she said softly.

Marc groaned. He smacked a palm to his temple. He should have known it. It was so obvious. She was the Polisario leader's woman. He felt the gorge rise in his throat. He got up and moved away from her.

"Does it matter to you?" she asked, as a fine blush deepened her coloring. How did he think she was able to move freely in and out of the Polisario camps? El-Ouali was her protector. The guerillas' vaunted policy of liberating women was mainly talk.

"You haven't been honest with me," he said wearily. How naïve he had been! No wonder El-Ouali detested him.

"What *are* your politics?" he asked finally, confronting her.

She glanced anxiously at the tent flap before she spoke. She was a socialist, but not the innocuous, run-of-the-mill variety. She belonged to the Marxist Twenty-third of March Movement, a radical band of young Moroccans who held out against the King on the Sahara. For her, the King and his form of government were an anachronism. She couldn't respect a country where a small wealthy elite manipulated the economy for their own purposes. She could believe in Polisario aims, if not its methods. As for the men in her life, they were not that important.

Marc weighed this bold sally. Probably in her mid-twenties, Aysha was neither as radical nor as jaded as she pretended to be. Like other "liberated" Arab women he had talked to, she claimed to have shucked every shackle of tradition. The transition was superficial. He leaned closer, aware of her faint musky scent.

"Haven't you ever cared for anyone? Is it all political?" he asked gently. He cared more about the answer than he wished to admit.

"Yes, I have cared...very much. Too much, perhaps." She spoke slowly now. "My fiancé, a leader of the Twenty-third of March movement, has been in a Moroccan prison for three years. He could be there for ten more." Her dark eyes misted. At last, he was getting the truth!

"Even he doesn't expect me to wait forever, but I have never become attached to anyone else. El-Ouali respects that."

She stood up, looking ill at ease and tired. The pain in her arm would have returned, he realized. Baring her soul had unnerved her. Aysha preferred her shroud of mystery.

"You must leave here," she said, brushing his forehead lightly with her fingers. She raised the woven door and disappeared.

Sickened, he lay back against the wall of goat hair. He was glad she was gone. He needed to be alone, to think. Her liaison with the fiery El-Ouali, who was obviously in love with her, and her duplicity from the beginning enraged him. How many men was she toying with with her Oriental wiles? Still, he was grateful for her warning.

She was that loyal to him. From the beginning, he had sensed hostility in the camp. Now Dr. Malki had been shunted off to the inferno of the prison camp. Poor devil!

But that wasn't what was eating at him now. For the first time in the camp, he was admittedly apprehensive. El-Ouali would kill him if he only suspected him of flirting with Aysha. No one tampered with an Arab's woman, especially if she belonged to an imprisoned hero. He didn't have the full story on the Polisario yet, but the time had come to make a move. It would not be easy. However, Aysha had given him a clue; the money sewn into his clothing might be the answer. He lifted the curtain and peered into the night.

Chapter Ten

The camp was quiet, the night was clear. He settled back on the straw mattress, Aysha's warning ringing in his ears. It was time to think things through.

He had a pretty good idea of how the camps were run, some idea of how the guerillas were trained. He had a first-hand report on the use of foreign advisors from the Cuban, Gonzalez. El-Ouali and Bashir had deluged him with Polisario thinking—he knew the propaganda by heart. Their aims were clear. He had strong impressions of the key figures, plenty of quotes and plenty of atmosphere from the denizens of the camp itself, whom he was certain came largely from regions other than the Spanish Sahara.

The only thing he lacked was proof of the Polisario capability. Dr. Malki's report on Soviet arms was useful, though he himself had seen nothing but a few Kalashnikovs. Nonetheless, he had enough to put together a whale of a series for the wire service. There would be freelance magazine articles in it, too, since no other American had visited the camps. Perhaps it was time to take Aysha's advice, to cut his losses and run.

He lifted the curtain and looked out again into the night. Against the desert horizon, the shadowy profile of the guard was outlined against a star-studded sky. Looking closer, he was started to recognize the squat shape, the listless stance. The gun was pointed carelessly at the man's foot. What abysmal luck! It was Mokhtar of the malevolent curse, whose twisted brain had pinned Marc as the devil, creator of sandstorms. Yet Aysha had persuaded Mokhtar to let her in the tent. Perhaps, in this case, a known quantity was preferable to the unknown.

Marc called to him softly, and the gun point swung in his direction. Mokhtar hesitated for a moment, then entered the tent. He looked almost professional now in the khaki worn by the elite guerilla cadres. His wide head was wrapped in the white *chèche*, its long end wound under his chin ready to be yanked over his nose against the blowing sand. Above it, the scar loomed like the scorch of a branding mark.

"*Podemos hablar?*" Marc tested Mokhtar's Spanish.

"*Sí.*" The gutteral response floated grudgingly in the night air. Mokhtar stared at the ground, yet his feelings toward Marc seemed less hostile. Had Aysha's bribe made an impression?

"So you speak Spanish?"

"*Naturalmente.*" Mokhtar shrugged like a hiccupping frog. He was a true Sahraoui from the Spanish territory, he said, not Algerian like the others. His spittle barely missed Marc's foot.

"Why then didn't you speak Spanish on the trip here?" Marc asked. Damn these devious people!

It was not wise to speak with a foreigner in a language the Algerians did not understand, Mokhtar murmured. Spanish was the colonizer's tongue. And they did not like secrets.

Marc smiled. The man should be congratulated on the degree of his unfriendliness toward foreigners.

"You let Aysha in the tent," he said.

"She gave me money. You didn't mind." It was the croak of a frog. So far so good. Marc nodded encouragingly and motioned to him to sit. Now their eyes were almost level. It was better that way, but they were not equals. The lanky American was still the prisoner, and he was aware of it.

"Tell me what they are saying about me in the camp," he said bluntly.

Mokhtar hesitated. Then his Spanish came forth in grunts. They didn't trust the American. He knew too much. They thought he would give a bad picture on the outside, because he was a spy. Baba heard it at the clinic.

So the chat with the Cuban paramedic had nailed him, Marc thought.

"Sometimes they torture spies," said Mokhtar blandly, peering to catch the other's expression of alarm.

Marc suppressed an impulse to seize him by the throat. He had to get to the point, before someone noticed that Mokhtar had left his post.

"Do you know a way out of the camp?" His nerves were taut as piano strings. He was placing himself at the mercy of the Sahraoui.

"Out of here?" Mokhtar pursed his lips and gave Marc a wide-eyed, know-nothing look. *He's faking,* Marc thought angrily. *He has something up his sleeve.*

"My escape to Morocco could prove worthwhile to you." He stared into Mokhtar's shifty eyes.

"I should turn you in, *amigo.*" The frog head bobbed righteously back and forth. *The wages of freedom,* thought Marc.

"I could pay you some now, more later," Marc said carefully.

"You have money! *Mucho mejor!*" Mokhtar's eyes flew open. "You give me one thousand dollars!" The comeback was too quick; he'd been planning it all along.

Marc said he didn't have a thousand dollars. If Mokhtar would suggest a plan, he would then make an offer. It was like haggling with a rug merchant in the medina, when in reality he was gambling for his life! At least he was not concerned about Mokhtar's loyalty to the Polisario. The man could be bought.

Mokhtar did have a plan. The National Council had decided to send Marc out with a motorized unit the next morning while they discussed his fate. It would be a routine sortie to prove how freely the guerillas roam the desert. They would show him abandoned Moroccan outposts, maybe some dead soldiers.

And how was he to get away from a band of armed guerillas?

The frog eyes bulged. This was the best of it. The *katiba* was led by a Cuban officer, a friend of Mokhtar. They often rode together, but he wouldn't go if Marc was along.

Abysmal logic! Marc's foot tapped impatiently on the ground.

Mokhtar continued to unfold his scheme. It was simple. The *americano* was not to know that Cubans organized the *katibas*. Therefore, on this particular day, the Cuban would not go out. The unit, composed of four Jeeps, was to leave at five a.m. They couldn't be caught because the Jeeps all traveled at the same speed—and nobody outdrove Mokhtar on the desert!

The plan was nightmarishly simple. Suppose an Algerian airplane was sent to track them down?

No such problem! Mokhtar would leave word that he took Marc to one of the other camps down south on orders from the Secretary-General. El-Ouali had left for Tindouf, a few hours earlier. That would put them off the track for a day.

"They trust me, because I say very bad things about you!" Mokhtar guffawed.

Marc looked admiringly at his improbable savior. The idea sounded plausible, but they would have to leave immediately. The Sahraoui's unshaven jaws creased in an obliging expression that might have been handsome in another face.

Three hundred U.S. dollars, one hundred now, two hundred when he was safely in Morocco. Marc waited for the roar of outrage. Bargaining was bargaining!

Mokhtar didn't disappoint him. His high-pitched squeal was that of a wounded boar. The scar moved to a vertical position. "*Hombre*! *Por dios*! I do not give my life for nothing. One thousand total."

The dickering continued. Marc held firm. He was not going to give Mokhtar all of the money that was stitched into his windbreaker and pants. At last, the deal was concluded for five hundred dollars, two hundred up front. But Marc had a question. Why did Mokhtar wish to leave the Polisario? Even if he fabricated the greatest lie on Earth, Marc wanted to hear it.

There was no hesitating this time. Life in the camp was hard. The food was rotten. The people became ill. They weren't even his people. It had taken five long months before the Polisario trusted him enough to go out on *katibas*. That was insulting!

For over ten years many Sahraoui like Mokhtar had been with

the Spanish *Tropas Nomadas*, a crack Bedouin fighting corps! When the Spanish left them stranded, they went over to the Polisario. They needed jobs and they feared Moroccan revenge, because they had served with colonial troops. Mokhtar had proved useful, he boasted. After a decade with the *Tropas*, he knew the Sahara like the back of his hand. He shoved his fist at Marc, naming its features: his knuckles were the ridge of Zemmour, the wide part of his hand was the great *hammada*; the spaces between his short, thick fingers were rivers and gorges.

The bulbous eyes turned fiery. Months before he had even carried out a dangerous job in Ceuta to the north. But the Polisario cheated him. They did not pay the Sahraoui as well as they paid Algerians and foreign mercenaries who knew nothing about the Spanish Sahara! Nor did they trust him. He was as much a prisoner as Marc was. If he attempted to visit his family in La Ayoun, he would be shot—or worse. A friend had been tortured to death for going home. With a furious snort, he stopped short.

Marc nodded. He understood the man better now. He hadn't lied. Hadn't the American ambassador tried months ago to persuade the King to take the discharged Sahraoui veterans into the Moroccan army? They would eventually cause trouble.

Mokhtar's eyes traveled around the tent. "*Vamos*! I talk too much. If someone sees I'm not out front, our plan is dead."

He got up. If the *señor* accepted his plan, he should be ready with the money at three-thirty a.m. The Jeep was stocked with extra gas and food. He scrambled from the tent.

In a few minutes he was back. He handed Marc a black bundle. The traditional *chèche*, a sort of turban, would envelop his face if he wore it as the Sahraoui did in the desert. Inside it was a pair of army fatigues belonging to Baba, who was still at the clinic. Mokhtar uttered a squeal of glee at this final touch.

Marc's fingers trembled as he set his watch by Mokhtar's. Mokhtar had devised a cunning plan. He knew the desert and was motivated. He wanted money and he wanted to go home. But he had few scruples and was quite capable of treachery. Marc thought of Aysha's parable of Justice. Moving about in the desert, he too was blind. Crossing the war zone, he would be at the mercy of his crafty guide. It was a gamble!

Yes, he wanted to escape this claustrophobic uncertainty—even if it meant losing touch with Aysha, who after all, in the camp at least, belonged to El-Ouali. The thought sickened him. What was her future? The Arab male was fickle. But she had made her own choice. Marc was in no position to interfere.

At three-thirty Mokhtar's whisper pierced the night.

"*Estás listo*? You have the money?"

Marc was ready. The black *chèche* covered his head. Only his eyes were visible through the narrow slit. He felt mummified, but even from a short distance, he would be taken for one of the guerillas. By a fluke, Baba was also tall and lean. The loose uniform fit well enough. He picked up his pack, a shirt wrapped around the medical kit and the almost-empty flask. These he would need. The suitcase he left behind; it would identify him immediately as a foreigner. In it were clothing and the cherished volume of Lawrence. It seemed a long time ago that he had sought its counsel. In the concealed pocket of his shorts, he felt a stiffness—a microscopic set of identity papers and the money he had had transferred from his clothing. He wouldn't see his passport or wallet again. They could be incriminating.

A nervous shiver shot through him as he slipped out of the tent, but he was relieved to see a pale early-hours moon, low on the dark horizon. He pressed two hundred-dollar bills into Mokhtar's waiting hand. With unhurried steps, they followed the barely visible path between dark, triangular blotches. Mokhtar waved confidently at a guard.

North of the encampment, they came on rows of parked Jeeps and Land Rovers, small trucks and armored cars. Hundreds of sand-colored bodies glowed in the soft moonlight. *Like a cemetery of open graves*, thought Marc. The Polisario were said to leave no corpses on the field of battle; the guerillas strapped themselves to their vehicles.

He wondered about a series of pyramids that glistened silver-white beyond. Shucking caution, he sprinted toward the ghostly piles, where stacked tubes clad with cases of white plastic caught the light. Missiles—probably 122 millimeter, he guessed. Nearby were rows of 50-caliber machine guns. Farther on, the lacy patterns of moon-lit steel were quadri-tubed anti-aircraft guns. The tubes protruding from platforms, like storks stretching from their nests, were multiple rocket launchers. Under a starlit canopy, the weapons had taken on an unearthly beauty. For a moment he ignored Mokhtar's frantic flailing arm and forced his mind to take notes. This depot was what he had not been shown. With such an arsenal, it was small wonder that the desert tribesmen needed advisors. No time to count them, just estimate the numbers. He saw the moving shadows of guards on duty and ducked behind a truck.

Approaching Mokhtar, he stopped in his tracks, startled to the point of panic. There was a distinct shadow in the back seat of the vehicle Mokhtar pointed to. Someone was waiting in it. For a terrorized moment, he considered a dash back to the security of his tent.

"*Está bien*," Mokhtar reassured him with a lecherous grin.

The small figure clad in loose white pants and shirt under a white turban slipped off a pair of Rommel sunglasses. Marc stared, incredulous. It was Aysha, beaming, ready for another grind across the desert. His heart skipped a beat on seeing her face. He pressed her hand, overwhelmed with relief. She was leaving with them.

Wordless, he climbed into the passenger seat. Then he felt the ground sliding from under him. A barrage of questions rattled through his head. Whose side was she on this time? Would she admit it if she were still working for El-Ouali? Had a jealous El-Ouali arranged to have her followed? What had she offered Mokhtar to convince him to take her along? Their chance of escape was already slim. Taking on a Polisario spy was like putting one's head in a lion's mouth. There were too many variables.

"What are you doing here?" he rasped. His impulse was to throw her out of the car.

In answer, she placed a finger to her lips. She was right. He fought against his rising ire. There was nothing to be done now. An argument was out of the question. The guards were too close.

Mokhtar slipped the Jeep into low gear, and the car moved away from the shadowy encampment. The crunch of tires on the *hammada*'s rough surface sounded like thunder to Marc's apprehensive ears. *Khatibas* left at irregular hours on different missions, Mokhtar assured him. Night was the best time to travel, if you knew the terrain. Aysha remained in the back seat, her long hair hidden under a white turban. She slouched low. Anyone seeing the Jeep would think that some sleepy young guerilla had been yanked from his tent for an early take-off. Marc didn't ask about her wound. He presumed she knew what she was doing.

Chapter Eleven

With sun-scorched eyes, Marc searched the desert for meaningful landmarks. To the left, gnarled fingers of dry rivers reached clawlike among sandy hummocks as if groping for something that wasn't there. Elsewhere nothing but occasional tufts of coarse yellow-green grass twisting around tangles of dried tamarisk bushes blown flat by the wind. For five hours the grumpy little Jeep had rattled over the pebble-strewn washboard of the *hammada*, sometimes achieving as much as thirty miles an hour, then falling back. Yet often it seemed to Marc that he was hurtling at breakneck speed. His insides felt mechanically churned by whirring blades. He wondered whether the guerillas had gotten used to it.

Were they heading north to Morocco, west to the sea or south to another Polisario camp? He felt absurdly dependent on Mokhtar's knowledge of the region. How long could the Sahraoui be trusted to perform according to plan? How long could they stay ahead of the Polisario? Or might they just have the luck to run smack into a clutch of mobile guerillas?

The sun had long since dispelled the chill of the night. As it began its scorching midday phase, its rays beat mercilessly on the open vehicle. The guerilla uniform provided by Mokhtar was proving its worth. The intricately folded *chèche*, piled high on his head, provided vital insulation. The widely curved dark glasses shielded his eyes from the blinding glare and flying particles. Men had lost their sight in the desert. It was no fable.

Without warning the Jeep shuddered to a halt near a flat-topped rock that protruded over a dry watercourse and afforded some shade. Mokhtar turned a skeptical eye on Marc. A wild cat was on the rampage in the *americano*'s stomach, no? They would eat, if he was able to. Cackling with hilarity, he leaned over the seat to rummage among the supplies.

"You get used to everything in this shitty desert!" he said.

Aysha stepped from the car. Her face was ashen and her eyes burned with intensity. She was being put to the test as much as he was, Marc thought. How tough was she really? If they fell into the hands of the Polisario, her defection would provoke dire consequences. Absconding with an infidel was unpardonable—unless of course she had come along to keep an eye on him! In answer to his questioning gaze, she turned abruptly to help Mokhtar with the food. She wasn't going to talk in front of the Sahraoui. It was just as well for the moment, but Marc smoldered with curiosity and a grating annoyance.

Aysha sat cross-legged under the sheltering rock with Mokhtar. Soon they were chatting in the Moroccan dialect of Arabic like old friends, while Marc looked on, disgruntled. A woman of mercurial moods, she could get on with anyone—when she cared to, he thought. Was he jealous of the Sahraoui? Ridiculous! After all, they shared a common background.

With queasy disinterest, he inspected a rocklike round of black bread and the soppy goat cheese that was already separating into yellow lumps. Under the rock Mokhtar was botching the job of opening a tin of sardines. Marc reached for the bottle of water, but the Sahraoui shook his head. Drinking during the day was ill-advised.

No relief! Marc took a short draught. His head whirling, he dropped to the ground to share the shade. They made an odd trio—a Bedouin guerilla, an American newsman and a defecting Polisario spy, each with a different motive for escape, each warily watching the other two, while feigning comradeship. Aysha continued her cheerful overtures to the Sahraoui. She was right. Mokhtar was in the driver's seat. For the present, he controlled their destinies.

Uninhibited by a mouthful of bread and cheese, Mokhtar waxed conversational. Sometimes he had feasted well in the desert. The guerillas hunted at dawn when gazelle, jackals and foxes were about. Such sorties livened up the long, bleak days. There were wells in the desert, too. One could count on them; it was against the Koran to foul the water.

Aysha explained. If one side was poisoned by the water, the other would be too. Water was sacred to the Bedouin, not only as necessary to life, but as the source of life. Wells were sacrosanct.

Despite the ache in his parched throat, Marc managed a grin. So there was a limit to treachery in the desert! Justice wasn't entirely blind. Aysha threw him a knowing glance.

Now Mokhtar removed the *chèche* from his dark curls and stretched prone on level ground. He pressed his bristly cheek in the sand, then returned to hard ground under the rock and listened again.

"*Nada*," he grunted. "If we are followed, they are not close. But we must move on." He was all business now, shaking out his fatigues and rewinding his turban as he spoke. For a moment Marc admired him. In his specialty he was a professional, putting to use what he had learned during a lifetime in the desert. Now after months of driving and training with the *katibas*, this was the day he had waited for.

Marc asked to know their present location. Mokhtar studied him suspiciously. Then he walked off and set about burying the remains of their lunch.

"Leave the driving to me," he growled over his shoulder.

Marc followed him, persisting, until Mokhtar explained in his grouchy, slow Spanish. They had started west toward the sea. Now they would turn north. It was not the route they had taken to the camp. The Polisario patrolled that one regularly.

They should pass Zag soon, Marc observed.

Mokhtar whirled at him. "*Nunca de la vida*! Do you think I am crazy? We are making a wide detour around the Moroccan outpost. Sure, Zag is totally isolated—without reinforcements, the soldiers don't normally go out in the desert. But if they see a lone Jeep, they will give chase and shoot. Zag will be of no use to you, just in case you are thinking of getting help there!"

He stamped angrily back to the Jeep before continuing. They would take the Ngueb Pass through the Ouarkziz Mountains to Tisgui Remz inside Morocco. Then they would cross the Draa Rivers and move east on to Assa. At Assa they would contact the Americans.

Marc agreed. They should penetrate well into Morocco before stopping. The Polisario scoured the border area periodically and they could be on the fugitives' tracks right now. If he was caught with an escaping guerilla, they might all be finished off then and there. People had disappeared in the desert before.

Marc insisted on taking a turn at the wheel, if only to make it patently clear to Mokhtar that he was neither helpless nor captive. The Sahraoui yielded grumpily, doggedly following Marc's every move with nervous eyes. Over the din of the motor, he shouted warnings and commands.

When they reached the edge of the *hammada*, Marc eased the Jeep slowly down the steep slope of an eroding gulch, trying to avoid causing a tell-tale avalanche of stones. A heap of debris could be seen hundreds of meters away. Soon he was following a vague track that was barely visible on the shifting sands of the open desert. Their own, well-grooved tire marks would be clearly defined for at least a day, unless the wind picked up. Tracking the Jeep would present no problem.

Ahead he saw a strange collection of dark shapes wobbling along the horizon.

O, God, they're on us! he thought.

Perhaps they were a mirage, like the pockets of blue water he had seen off and on since dawn. They turned out to be real.

"You can count the bodies if it gives you pleasure!" Mokhtar's grim laugh resounded above the motor. This was the result of a surprise attack on a Moroccan relief column. They were probably en route to join the garrison at Mahbes, he said.

"I'll circle once," Marc said tersely. If it hadn't been important to his story, he'd have avoided the grisly chore. With all his years of reporting, he'd never become inured to corpses.

Settled among the drifting dunes, the remains of a dozen vehicles were interspersed with battered pieces of artillery. It was apparent that anything worth salvaging had been carted off by the Polisario. It was also apparent that the retreating Moroccans had moved out too fast to remove their dead. Green-uniformed bodies, some strapped in the vehicles, others scattered at random on the sand, had been partially devoured by jackals. Now a flock of brown buzzards bickered nastily over the remains.

Marc felt nauseous. War in the desert was as ugly as anywhere else. He was relieved to see Aysha dozing peacefully in the back seat.

Farther on, they came on a fighter plane. Half buried under the sand, it might have been a mechanical toy that had glided off on its own and eventually coasted down to rest, forgotten by its owner.

"*Mira, Marco!* An American plane. The SAM got him!"

It was an old American-made F-5. The pilot had been Moroccan, of course, since the Algerians used Soviet MiGs. Perhaps it was the man he had spoken to at the camp, or perhaps this one hadn't survived. His desiccated body might be lying around somewhere. Another horrid reminder that even this limited war, scarcely known to the outside world, was takings its regular toll.

The afternoon was turning torrid when a long, treeless escarpment shimmered into view, dancing in wavy lines along the horizon. As they approached, it slowly solidified and rose like a great reddish wave, curling and ready to break over the ochre wasteland. The Ouarkziz range was well within Morocco and thus the border was near.

Perhaps they had crossed the border when Mokhtar directed Marc toward a rocky promontory. Behind it curved an amphitheater of pillared walls. Under the striated, red-brown rock, a dark smudge looked like the mouth of a cave. Mohktar's hand shot out in front of Marc and, in response, he stopped the car.

"*Cuidado!*" Mokhtar's whisper was a command for silence. He seized a flashlight and jumped from the Jeep, cautioning Marc and Aysha to remain in the car. Stealthy as a jackal, he slipped along the wall toward the cave. Soon they could see the glow of his flashlight as it swept the interior.

"We can stay here," he said, emerging at last.

"My impression was that we were driving to Assa!" Marc barked, his suspicions kindled anew. His head whirled from sheer heat.

"*Ahora no es posible!*" Mokhtar shot back angrily. "Driving north is dangerous in daylight. We will be fired upon by Moroccan border patrols. Or the Polisario. It is also the hottest time of day. We will benefit by resting."

Marc agreed reluctantly. The cave yawned invitingly, a refuge from the fiery inferno. He was having trouble connecting his thoughts, having barely slept during the night. It was true that their Polisario Jeep moving through the high Ouarkziz would make a perfect target. The Moroccans would shoot first and ask questions after. But now they were on the edge of no-man's land, where the Polisario also lurked. Their track through the desert led directly to the cave. Either way involved risk.

He helped the dazed, unrecognizable Aysha from the Jeep. Like a gnome from another planet in the ballooning white pants and turban worn by the Polisario, now chalky with fine powder, she stumbled ahead of him toward the cave, too exhausted to speak. Moving into the dank interior behind her, Marc felt a pleasurable tingling relief pervade his body, as though he had plunged head-first into a cool pool. Gratefully, he spread his tired limbs on bare ground. His appetite had returned, and he gladly accepted a portion of Mokhtar's previously unappetizing provisions. As his eyes adjusted to the dim interior, he noted ashes of previous fires. Litter was disturbingly visible in a far corner of the cave. It had been recently used, probably by the Polisario. But he was too tired to speculate on the various scenarios that thought brought to mind. For now, he wished only to sleep. Mokhtar was right.

Hours later Marc awoke to total darkness. He shook his head groggily. He was alone, but someone was speaking outside. He crept to the entrance. Peering into the gathering night, he saw Aysha standing by the Jeep. Her dark eyes stared in his direction, tense and unnatural. Was she preparing some sort of get-away? Then he realized that she was motioning to him to go back into the cave. At that moment a figure leapt from the shadow beside the cave entrance. He found himself looking into the barrel of a pistol framed by Mokhtar's shaggy head.

"*Dentro!*" Mokhtar brandished the weapon, and Marc backed into the cave with raised hands.

Mokhtar advanced, muttering in monosyllabic Spanish. Marc was to stay inside the cave. If he moved toward the Jeep, Mokhtar would shoot both him and the woman. Alone he had brought the two of them through the desert. Now he would drive alone over the mountain range to the town of Assa, where he would telephone the Americans. For delivering Marco Lamont, he would demand the five thousand dollars he deserved.

Marc howled in protest. No one would believe Mokhtar. It was a ridiculous amount of money. Without proof, he wouldn't receive a penny.

Oh, Lord, he prayed, *let me get through to this man.*

Mokhtar waved the pistol toward the mountains in a gesture of futility. Escape for the two of them was out of the question. If the Moroccans saw them, they would open fire; only the Polisario roamed this area. In the desert they would surely lose their way and die. And if they fell into the hands of the Polisario, their lives would be worth *nada*. "*Nada!*" he shrieked again, the sounds rising and falling like the whistle of a passing express.

"Stop!" Marc bellowed. "You don't know who to call!" He took a pad from the medical kit and wrote in large figures the number of the American Embassy in Rabat. "The name to ask for is important. Few people know who I am. You talk to McGonigal. No one else."

"Ma gonna kill, ma gonna kill!" Mokhtar mumbled, aping him.

Marc seethed. What simple-minded greed! The Sahraoui was naïve and unrealistic. He'd never get the money on his own. But he had a gun. Why risk Aysha's life, as well as his own, by trying to stop him? There were no reasonable half-measures in all this. There were no grays in the desert, only black and white.

He walked out of the cave and approached the Sahraoui, his eyes locked on the others'. Then he imposed his own conditions. Mokhtar should realize that if he abandoned Aysha and him in the cave, the Americans would find out. They would trace him and find him. Mokhtar would get jail, not money. Thus, if he did not come back within forty-eight hours, Marc would not help him obtain the money they had agreed upon. They had a bargain—Mokhtar had to live up to his end. Furthermore, if Mokhtar helped Marc, the Moroccans would be convinced of his sincerity as a defector from the Polisario. Marc would back him up. Otherwise, they might assume that he was still working for the other side.

Marc glared with a ferocity that forced Mokhtar to look away. The muscle-flexing was a bit of bravado and he knew it.

Mokhtar shrugged, grudgingly. "*Quizás sí, Quizás no!* Only do not move now. I left some food. I return tomorrow." He pushed Aysha aside, climbed into the Jeep, and with a grinding of gears, the vehicle vanished in a cloud of dust.

"There's your lesson on justice in the desert!" Aysha grimaced, as though she had predicted this latest turn of events.

"Lesson! I've had nothing but lessons from you and that damned gorilla!" Marc blurted.

"Marc, don't worry. We're lucky! We made it through the desert. We're in Morocco!" She flung out her arms on both sides in pure elation, cutting a comical, gamine figure in her strange rig. "Mokhtar will do it for the money, if nothing else," she added, her body moving toward the cave with animal grace under the loose Polisario garb.

Sweet reasoning! Marc cursed himself silently, for having slept so long, for allowing himself to be fooled by the Sahraoui, for being stranded in a no-man's land—with no possibility of getting in touch with the wire service. Mokhtar was simple-minded perhaps, but cagey and as tough as any Reguibat. Now he had the upper hand.

And Aysha? She, too, was a creature of the desert. Astonishingly resilient, she was as nonchalant as ever, happy to be back in Morocco. Would he finally get the truth from her now that they were alone?

Doubts plagued him. If they were tracked to the cave, she could turn him back to the Polisario—as her catch. His fate in the Sahara seemed as fragile as a sand dune in a gale.

Chapter Twelve

Aysha gazed at the distant horizon, where undulating ochres and tans melted into ultramarine. A star came to life, a pin prick of pure light. Nothing else really. Two fields of color melting into each other, an abstraction of blue and brown. No sign of man marred its vast emptiness. Yet the desert was no lifeless vacuum, she mused. Foxes, badgers and other burrowing beasts were testing the night with inquisitive noses; serpents were slithering forth on noctural sorties. And somewhere out there, the Polisario were sprawled by their vehicles, waiting out the night.

Marc sat down beside her in front of the cave, his limbs entwined, long arms cradling long legs. The lines of his features were blurred with fine dust. A layer of skin flaked from the sunburned nose. His thick eyebrows were caked with sand, his hair bleached with light powder. She liked him this way, weather-softened, the sharp edges blunted, like the wavelets of sand that rippled away from them.

For the first time since she had known him, he wasn't in racing gear. For the moment his feisty drive was stalled, stymied by the Sahraoui, and she rather liked that, too. For now, briefly, he belonged to her. She had tossed herself over a precipice for this stranger. Fate had thrown them together and, inevitably, fate would separate them again. She must steel herself against his attractiveness.

A cool night breeze skipped through his stiffly matted brush of hair. His furrowed brow seemed intent on piercing the horizon, but a barely perceptible rocking motion gave him away. Aysha sensed his impatience, his demand for an open confession, American-style. But life had schooled Aysha differently. Self-revelation was not her style. She preferred her veil of secrecy.

"Do you want to talk?" he said at last, almost belligerently.

Aysha was only too aware that his image of her was that of a changeable, fickle creature. Was he capable of understanding her? Would he recognize the forces that had driven her by turns to take certain steps?

"Yes, actually, I do. I need to think about it a little." She paused, looking out over the darkening sand.

"I know so very little about you. Yet this is the second time I've placed my trust in you. You've got to understand that I need to know what motivates you, why you are behaving as you do," he said, adding, "Where do you stand, Aysha? What do you really believe in?"

"I have to go back to the beginning. There are so many things I never told you, or even hinted at." She hesitated. "Perhaps this one fact is especially vital. I didn't tell you that my grandmother was a black slave."

Marc's head flipped toward her as she continued in low tones.

"Long ago my grandmother told me how she was brought by caravan from Senegal. She was only a small child. Six or seven, no more. In Marrakech she was sold to a plantation-owner, my grandfather, whose groves of oranges lay south of Agadir. There she grew up in the household among a number of domestic servants from areas south of the Sahara. She was pretty. She was very clever. Inevitably, of course, when she was in her teens, she was placed in the harem."

She saw his surprise. "That happens to all of them. In a way, it's a form of protection. There are guards—eunuchs. No one gets in but the master of the house. I mean a servant, a person of low status, can be set upon by anybody. Women have little defense against rape in this country, you know.

"My grandfather was much older—twenty-five years older—but incredibly, it was a true love affair. She adored him. And he, her. Black concubines were much coveted in Morocco, even in the royal household. I suppose they still are. Black blood runs in the most aristocratic families." She laughed.

"It is believed that these women possess magical secrets and great sexual prowess. They say that their love potions bend a man's will and make him servile. On the other hand, even today, their sorcery is feared. A hex on a man will make him impotent!"

"Good God, don't put one on me!" he exclaimed.

"Don't tempt me!" she parried and continued. "Anyway, through her wiles and charms, or more probably her basic intelligence, my grandmother ascended to the position of 'Favorite.' In the end, my grandfather married her. She became the most important of the four wives of course, being at that time the youngest and most beautiful. She came to live in the family palace in Fez.

"She was a wonderful woman, a tremendous personality. She told me endless stories about the intrigues that constantly bedevil life in a harem. Some of them are very funny. And in that great house, believe me, she ran the show." Aysha swayed with the telling, relishing her story. Then her tone changed.

"But beneath that gaiety there was a certain sadness. My grandmother never knew who her people were or where she was born." Her voice tapered off before she resumed speaking.

"Her name was Aysha. I was her namesake—and I felt a special kinship with her because I, too, was taken from home. After the earthquake in Agadir, I was sent to live with my uncle's family in Fez when I was still very young. Because of that I had a chance to know her.

"At my grandmother's knee, I learned that women live in a world created by men for the pleasure of men. I learned how we are hemmed in by layers of walls. The walls of tradition, yes centuries of tradition, are as thick and as high as the walls that surround our cities and our homes. I learned that woman survives by guile, by her brains alone, because she has no other resources. If she is strong, she rules supreme within the home; she is its master. As you know perhaps, it is possible that after her marriage she may never leave its walls.

"Anyway, once she married, my grandmother never left the two rooms assigned to her in the palace. But her power reached way beyond those walls. She achieved it by dominating the men in her life—her husband, her sons, her brothers-in-law. She learned early not to trust any man. Did you know that that is the basic lesson we learn—never to surrender our power by loving too much. It is sad, don't you think?"

Marc remained silent, listening, nodding his head.

"You in the outside world, you have little idea of how our lifestyle has molded the character of our women—in unexpected ways. Even today a man tends to put his wife in a little box or a frame separate from the rest of his life. Thus we are forced to be highly disciplined. We have to find ways to realize our hopes within the parameters given us. In the end, what happens? Women have more strength of character than men and more courage. And today, we are receiving an education that is equal to a man's.

"But, don't mistake me, we also know that, as we change with the times, it is not necessary to turn against Islam. It doesn't matter whether we wear blue jeans or the veil, or even if we have jobs. We can still believe in Islam."

"Okay, I'll buy it. But it's a pretty tough role, Aysha," he said slowly. "Tell me how all this affects you."

Aysha drew herself up, leaning toward him.

"Even recently, Muslim women did not learn to read and certainly did not learn foreign languages. I shattered family tradition. Not only by going to school—that is, the French *Lycée*—but by moving on to the University of Rabat. That was blasphemous. And I had to fight for it. Even worse, I was rejecting the mores of my family. It seemed to me that the wealthy elite of Fez were simply furthering the degradation of their own women. I assure you, I wanted to get out. I longed for some other way of life. So I went to Europe to study.

"Well, it was in Geneva when I was at the translating school— that's where I learned English—I fell in with a group of Marxists. Oh, they appealed to me! They preached a total break with the past, you know. This went far beyond anything I'd thought of before. For many of the students, talking and dreaming was enough. But not for me. I wanted to be a part of it. You see I thought I was learning a better way of life, not just for me, but for Morocco. The time was near when the rich would no longer bilk the poor, when women would cast off their shackles.

"So I returned to Fez and joined the militant *Frontistes*—you've heard of them, the most radical of the radicals. They were clamoring for government reform. Well, no Moroccan king has ever tolerated active dissent, and King Hassan is no exception! When some of the demonstrations got out of hand, many of my colleagues—some still in their teens—were sent to prison. My fiancé was a leader, a man of real spirit and fire. He was sentenced to an indefinite term. That was three years ago. The movement in Morocco was effectively stifled."

Marc was very quiet now, staring at the stars. So incredibly bright they were in the blue-black canopy.

"I'm not boring you, am I?" she asked. "Shall I go on?"

"Yes, yes. I want to hear it all. Please go on," he said.

"So, a year ago in Morocco, I met another group of young men with a very special cause. The Bedouin of the Western Sahara were to be saved from annexation by Morocco. An ideal democratic state, in which women would be the equal of men, was in the making. That's when I met the leader of the group, El-Ouali Mustapha Sayed. To me, he was really dazzling! He was so passionately idealistic. He seemed so capable. He became my Che Guevara.

"And so I secretly joined the Polisario Front. My job was to pick up information in Casablanca and Rabat and relay it, while posing as a translator. Actually I like that. I mean the double role. It's a bit like the game played behind the doors of the harem, if you know what I mean. A kind of power play. You have to be clever—and sometimes, a little bit deceitful."

Marc heaved a sigh. "What you've been through!" He shook his head, his gaze still glued to the horizon. "I guess what you've done is to exchange a tangible veil for an intangible veil. You seem pretty determined to revenge yourself on a society that keeps women in chains," he said.

She realized that he was still waiting. He wasn't letting her off the hook. She had to go through to the end.

"I suppose disillusion was bound to follow. Lately, I found I've been making excuses for the Polisario—for the leadership, I mean. I couldn't help but see that the deeds didn't match the words. Their methods are difficult to reconcile with the ideal. For example, they want to impress the world with the greatness of their cause, so thousands of refugees have been recruited from drought-stricken Sahel countries to the south. It's just a way to swell the numbers in the camps. Their children are forced to learn Spanish, so that they can be passed off as Saharans. You saw that, I think. For a long time I told myself it was for a worthy cause.

"Only on this trip I finally learned how far they've gone. El-Ouali bragged about a new Soviet weapon he had acquired from Libya. This machine fires several missiles at once—a distance of twenty kilometers. They truck it all over the desert. In fact, East German instructors are training the guerillas to use it."

Marc whistled softly.

"Hey, wait a minute! That's what I saw outside the camp—the round platforms with the tubes."

She nodded. "They're called 'Stalin Organs.' At that moment it dawned on me that these advanced weapons would be used against my own countrymen, who don't have anything to retaliate with. And then El-Ouali began to talk about the new SAM 9 missile. He boasted—these are his very words—that he and his brother 'came to Libya barefoot.' At the time they had no backing in the Sahara or anywhere else. They were just a group of disgruntled university students studying in Rabat. When they returned from Libya with a generous promise of arms, the Polisario Front was made."

Marc looked at her, amazed. "Has it occurred to you that this phoney little war may be nothing but a testing ground for Soviet hardware—delivered by Qadhafi?"

"It's starting to sink in. You have to understand that at one time I sincerely believed in the Polisario—and everything they stood for," Aysha said ruefully. "Well, after I learned about the Stalin Organ, I began to make sense of overheard conversations. The picture I was piecing together was a new one, and I didn't particularly like Qadhafi's role in it."

"I agree," said Marc. "God only knows how far his designs extend. And it becomes pretty clear why the Algerians are harboring the Polisario. First, the new puppet state will give them access to the Atlantic Ocean—to ship their iron ore, and other products, around the world. Secondly, they thus surround Morocco by land. And eventually, with their superior military power, they just might cause its government to collapse. This K.O.s the balance of power in North Africa,

"Aysha, it's obvious. The Sahraoui cause is a tool. It has nothing to do with self-determination or independence for anybody. The region doesn't have the raw materials to sustain a viable economy. I've got a story all right." He grinned. Then he turned back to Aysha.

"But, hold on, let's just go back for a minute to the personal side of things. So you were disenchanted, right? I can swallow that. And I provided the means to get out. Is that it?" His eyes were probing hers. The confession wasn't finished.

Back to Mustapha El-Ouali. Was he a fallen idol or did he still command her? How to say it? She faltered and began again.

"You remember when we first lunched together in Rabat? Well, I suppose I can admit it. I thought you might be favorably impressed by the Polisario. Certainly you were in a position to advance their cause. My plan was simply to bring you to the camp. When I told Mustapha, that is, El-Ouali about it, he jumped at the idea—at first. Yet when I arrived with you, he seemed to go crazy. I'll never forget it—the image of his face suddenly purple and terrifying. He had a whip, Marc. He threatened me. If he hadn't been called away and actually had to leave the camp, he might have killed me.

"You do not know how possessive Arab men can be. For the first time, I was utterly terrified—yet it was all so unnecessary." Aysha stopped short. "You see, I was never his mistress." She met Marc's gaze straight on, knowing that at last he believed her.

"Oh, yes, Mustapha El-Ouali thought of me as his private property, but I did not give in. *Never!* I knew, I guess, that I was playing with fire. For over a year I had idolized him as a 'brother' in the party, but I knew instinctively that...that he was capable of brutality. He assumed, of course, that one day we would be lovers. And as far as anyone in the camp was concerned, I was reserved for him. Apparently, after I arrived with you, Said talked to him.

"Said resented my favored position. I had more influence with Mustapha than he, more freedom to come and go. Said knew how to ruin me—just a hint at my relations with you and El-Ouali was on fire. He'd never forgive—nor forget—losing face because of me!"

Marc did not look at her. He was busily sketching something in the sand with bold, hard strokes. Aysha sensed his thoughts. He still wasn't satisfied. She began again.

"As for you, it has taken me a long time to understand you at all. I didn't know why you came here. I always suspected some other reason. But I began to trust you and understand that you came here because you felt it was important to know the truth—not to be a hero, not for revenge, not for personal gain. You simply wanted to know the story of my people." She felt herself blushing.

"I dallied with you at first, because I was attracted to you. You came from another life. So, in a way, you were safe. There would be nothing permanent. But it became more than that... "

Abruptly, Marc seized her waist and threw her with all his strength away from him. She tumbled awkwardly on her bad arm, bruising her hand. Surprised and hurting, she glanced back to see him flailing the ground with a stick. Then the beam of his flashlight moved over the area where she had been sitting.

"A viper! Sorry! I didn't mean to hurt you." He moved toward her, scouring the ground. "Thank God I saw it! It's dead now."

She gasped. The lacerated body of the snake, light gray, stippled with brown, was still writhing, its sharp little horns pointing in her direction. The bite of the venomous *lefsa* was lethal. It was the reptile most feared by the Sahraouis!

She stood up shakily to thank Marc, aware that she had been totally absorbed in her narrative. How could she have forgotten that in the desert man was only one menace among many? Perhaps the interruption was a blessing. Should one tell everything about oneself? She busied herself making a bundle of the twigs she had collected earlier.

"Aysha! Aysha!" Marc murmured later inside the cave, staring into the leaping flames of the fire they had started. "Passionate, wildly impulsive and like a sharp-clawed panther, impossible to subdue. What is the Aysha myth? You never told me about it. Are you endowed with special powers?"

She laughed, welcoming the light touch.

"According to ancient legend, Aysha Kandicha is the wife of the devil. She lures men to their deaths, You can recognize her by her goat hooves. See!" Aysha stretched her own dusty but well-formed extremities for inspection.

"Your feet are perfect, just like the rest of you. But you can't convince me that you're a normal mortal, a mere woman like any other." He was only half-joking.

"I won't try," she said. "Aysha Kandicha is libidinous and lustful— and so am I!" She brushed his cheek with her lips.

"One thing still stumps me. How did you know that I was leaving the camp? How did you learn about Mokhtar's plan?" he parried.

"Mokhtar's plan?" She lifted an eyebrow. Sometimes he could be very dense. "Do you really believe that Mokhtar would have the imagination and the guts to make off with a Polisario vehicle, unless someone put him up to it?"

"Not Mokhtar's plan," he said slowly, his lips widening into a self-mocking grin. "Why didn't I catch on? Of course, you put him up to it!"

"I had to get out myself. It seemed so obvious. There was no other way." Her smile was almost apologetic.

"Mokhtar would never have agreed to take me away alone. The Bedouin are suspicious of lone women. He would never understand that I require freedom as much as a man might. Even for money he wouldn't have done it. An American was another matter. It was a worthy job!"

"You think we can trust Mokhtar?" he asked.

"No!" she said soberly. "But he wants the money. If he calls the Embassy, somebody will come after us, won't they?"

Marc pulled her gently toward him. "I don't like to admit it, but if I get out of this place and get my account published, I'll owe the whole thing to you."

"You're not out of it yet," she said, examining his sun-blistered face. The desert had changed him, scuffed him up a bit. He had slowed down. He was listening and he was thinking. When he put his arms around her, she wondered whether these would be their last moments alone.

Marc awoke later. He had heard something. He sensed a presence and reached for Aysha. She was gone. He looked up and saw to his surprise a face he despised. He could never forget it, because he had committed it to memory. Even in the dim light from the dying embers, he could recognize the leering mouth with its deformity. Its breath was putrid. The harelip from Marrakech!

The nephew of the man who tried to assassinate the King! El-Ouali had sent his murderer, Oufkir, after them. For an instant, their eyes were locked together with mutal hatred. Then, inexplicably, Oufkir lurched and whirled back toward the cave entrance. The pistol he held swerved with him. Two shots ricocheted off the walls, almost drowning a muffled cry.

Aysha! She had drawn him away.

In a fraction of a second, Marc leapt upon him, kicking the gun off into the darkness and pulling him to the floor. Behind Oufkir, he saw a bloodied knife fall and spin to one side. The heavy Moroccan, infuriated by the sudden pain, rolled on top of Marc, seizing his shoulders. His fingers clawed for Marc's throat. Marc tensed his muscles for a karate thrust. Gasping for breath, he heaved the thick bulk off him and groped around in the dark for the knife.

Oufkir was ahead of him. He seized the knife and came at Marc again, the blade a flicker of orange from the embers. Marc scrambled to his feet. He felt the breath of the other man engulf him, as Oufkir lunged. Marc's knee caught him full in the stomach, knocking him sideways on the floor. One leg landed on the live embers. With a shriek of pain, Oufkir dropped the weapon. Marc fell to his knees, groping where he had seen the blade's glitter. As his fingers closed around the leather handle, Oufkir leapt again. When Marc made a blind thrust, Oufkir's arms were closing around him in a vice. Frenziedly, Marc twisted the knife handle. It seemed that whole minutes passed while they lay locked together. Marc was dimly conscious of being crushed by the other man's weight. Abruptly, the pinioning arms fell loose. Oufkir's last cry ended in a strident rattle as his arms flailed the ground and fell limp. Marc rolled the body off him and sprang woozily to his feet.

He called to Aysha. An eerie echo came back to him. He could see nothing. He searched for the packet of matches with which he had started the fire. Fighting to control his trembling fingers, he struck several on the ground, wasting them. At last he had a flame. He picked up an overturned candle, lit it and swept the flickering light in an arc. Aysha was lying near the entrance. Breathless, he fell on her and lifted her head in his hands.

Aysha's eyes flew open, wide with terror.

"Where is he?" she cried.

She was not hurt. The bullets had gone wild. Oufkir had flung her against the rock wall, and she had fallen unconscious.

With a deep sigh of relief, Marc returned to Oufkir's twisted body, avoiding the widening pool of blood under his right side. He grasped a wrist and felt for the trace of a pulse, then placed an ear on the gaping mouth.

Turning to Aysha, he said limply, "It's all over!"

His brain reeled. He had never killed a man. The fight had left him faint, but a strange primal joy surged within him. He had vowed to track down the renegade bully who had assaulted him—and how many others? He had succeeded, but he hadn't done it alone.

"You saved my life," he said softly.

"It was you or him," she answered groggily, adding, "Allah has decreed that every man must lose his life!"

"So be it. Where did you find the knife?" he asked, unwinding the turban which had protected her head when she fell.

"Mokhtar hid it in the Jeep before we left camp. I saw him," she answered. "He thought I would be on his side. It never occurred to him that a woman might act on her own! Before he left, I slipped it in with the food. Tonight I heard a motor and took it with me outside the cave. Oufkir never saw me."

"You had the nerve to attack Oufkir!" he exclaimed, dumbfounded.

He turned to Oufkir's body and uttered a few words—a prayer, or perhaps an incantation. Still panting, he grasped the blood-soaked corpse by the heels and dragged it to the cave entrance. He must bury it at once and cover the traces. Polisario vengeance would be swift.

Chapter Thirteen

Marc and Aysha emerged from the cave as the first pink light began to bathe the desert in pastel. Crest after sandy crest, a mosaic of brown turning coral with the early light, then tan. Behind them, the flank of rock, sepia in color and striated with darker slate, was ever poised to break like a wave over the desert. Overhead, a brown buzzard, circling purposefully, displayed its pink underbelly. Then it dove at a crevice, its powerful beak thrust forward. For an instant, it grappled with a lizard. The reptile's legs jerked helplessly, then disappeared, swallowed in a gulp. Aysha shuddered. Nature was harsh, Marc thought. In the open car, they would also be easy targets.

Oufkir's Jeep was intact, the keys in the ignition. A jerry can was wedged behind the back seat. He had intended a swift departure. Marc smiled. The assassin's arrival was a blessing in disguise. They didn't have to wait for the return of Mokhtar, whose tire marks were still clear, leading eastward on the sand. But heading north into the mountains, they would have to find their way. Marc wondered whether the thin mist shrouding the jagged ridge above concealed a hostile force. In this zone, one side would be as trigger-happy as the other. On the radio antenna, he hung a frayed remnant of white shirt, a makeshift truce flag. Aysha nodded approval.

"Say a prayer and keep your eyes open. I have to watch the track," he said, turning the ignition key with nervous fingers.

"Even if we get through, this will be the end for us. It could be jail for me," she said, her eyes a shade too bright.

"Don't think about it," he replied without looking at her. "We just don't know what the future holds."

Shortly after dawn, they left the desert where a track led into the mountains. Painfully, the Jeep labored, climbing steadily between high limestone ramparts. Marc presumed that they were in the Ngueb Pass. There was no way of knowing, and the going was proving more treacherous than he had imagined. A flat tire would be a disaster. He was ruing the fact that he hadn't checked for tools when he heard a high-pitched whistle above his head. Ducking under the wheel, he pulled Aysha roughly to the floor with him.

The Jeep veered sideways and stalled, blocking the road. A hail of bullets had passed over. In a moment the patrol was upon them. Two soldiers in green uniforms advanced with cocked guns. Others were visible behind a partially concealed gun emplacement. Marc breathed a sigh of relief. He was drenched with sweat. It had been a close encounter.

"Moroccans! We should be okay," he said, sitting up cautiously.

Although they had showered him with bullets each time he passed the border, the dusky green uniforms of the Royal Armed Forces were a welcome sight. Aysha called out in Arabic. The soldiers kept their guns on the ready. Once abreast of the Polisario Jeep, the doughty troopers stared. The small Moroccan woman in Polisario whites and the tall, disheveled foreigner in dusty khakis didn't look like guerillas. Surely they weren't tourists!

One of the soldiers ordered Marc out of the Jeep and roughly frisked him, while a rude exchange broke out between Aysha and the other Moroccan. With a catlike hiss, she refused to be touched. The embarrassed oaf was no match for her. She insisted that they be taken to the *gendarmerie* at Assa. That was fine by him.

The soldiers moved quickly now, concerned that the Jeep may have been set up as a Polisario ambush. Marc and Aysha were brusquely escorted to an armored car parked behind a crag. A soldier climbed into the Jeep, and shortly the two vehicles were grinding up the pass between crenelated battlements of pink rock. In the rear of the car, two yawning recruits who couldn't have been more than fifteen years old eyed Marc and Aysha with curious distrust. Allah deserved a prayer of thanks, Marc mused. They had escaped the Polisario, crossed the desert, killed Oufkir, evaded Mokhtar and the bullets of the Moroccans. If they had survived up to this point, all should be well. Furthermore, no one would have to pay Mokhtar a penny for his treachery.

Beyond the pass, on the flatland again, the small motorcade rumbled through Tisgui Remz, a hamlet of adobe huts that seemed to have sprung from the Old Testament. No children scurrying barefoot, no women hiding under tightly-drawn black shawls, however; its denizens had fled the war zone. Another twenty-five miles of rutted track passed through desolate scrubland. Here and there, they spied the towers of *kasbahs*, the famed fortress-castles built of mud and straw, crumbling in ruins and as bleached as seashells. At last they arrived at the sun-baked cluster of adobe structures that comprised Assa. Set among wind-ravaged palms, it had the abandoned look of a Pueblo village. Or, thought Marc, a Picasso canvas of Cubist shapes. Not a creature stirred under the blazing sun. A faded flag fluttered over the *Gendarmerie*, its green star barely discernible on the rust-colored field.

"Glad to see the Moroccan colors again?" Marc asked Aysha. For an instant he seized her hand. She returned the pressure.

"I love my country," Aysha said softly. "I never changed sides. It wasn't as simple as that."

As if in response to these remarks, three Moroccan *gendarmes*, pistols drawn, charged from the building and flung open the rear door of the armored car. The two teenagers were shoved aside. Sparks of sunlight glinted off the snub-nosed firearms pointed at the strangers in guerilla garb.

"*Merikani!*" Aysha added a torrent of Arabic.

"Just obey them!" Marc said curtly. "A Polisario Jeep arriving in a Moroccan town in broad daylight is a bit of a shock. They'll be more confused when they try to figure out what a wandering American and a Moroccan woman in guerilla garb have been doing in the Ouarkziz.

"Whatever you do, don't hawk the fact that I'm a reporter or I'll never get out of here. For the moment, I'm hoping for some sort of immunity." He touched her hand again reassuringly.

Within the *Gendarmerie*, an army captain surveyed the new arrivals over a sloping paunch. He looked tired of the war, the mess and confusion, and particularly the airless cubicle that served as his office. He asked for identity papers.

Struggling with the lining of his jacket, Marc produced a microscopic set of credentials, which the captain examined suspiciously. At intervals, he stared at the newcomers, squint-eyed, like a curious tortoise whose tranquil lagoon had been invaded.

Marc explained that Colonel Dlimi, Chief of Moroccan Security, should have been informed of his disappearance, hoping that the CIA chief had reported him missing. The American Embassy would verify his story—just to get him back. Fortunately, Morocco was a country friendly to the U.S. An hour passed while the captain consulted with underlings, gave instructions and shouted sporadically into the telephone. Marc gritted his teeth, summoning patience. His experience had taught him that no bureaucrat in this part of the world responded with alacrity to the unforeseen. Furthermore, any hint that he might be reporting Moroccan reverses in the desert would land him in limbo for good.

Then the door opened to reveal a shabby figure escorted by soldiers. Marc scarcely recognized Mokhtar, who had shed the guerilla uniform and now appeared in a soiled T-shirt and dark pants. His head thrust forward, eyes wild, lips moving mechanically, he resembled a boar at bay. Damn him! Mokhtar had obviously made a mess of things.

Aysha whirled at him furiously. In the ensuing exchange, Marc caught a few words. Before being stopped by a patrol, Mokhtar had made a call to the American Embassy, probably from the home of a dissident friend. Now he was concocting improbable lies for the Moroccans. He had betrayed them, she charged.

Mokhtar fought back. The American had cheated him. He owed Mokhtar money. The livid scar worked furiously through the bristles on his cheek.

The captain rumbled into the fray which had now become a three-ring circus, featuring the elephant, the clown and the trapeze artist.

Marc thundered in French. "The Sahraoui is a Polisario guerilla. He's not to be trusted! One telephone call to Colonel Dlimi or to the American Embassy will settle everything. If the captain doesn't make that call now, I will use my diplomatic influence to have him stripped of rank!"

This bit of bravado seemed to stick, since, for the moment, Marc was an unknown quantity. The uproar ceased. The reptilian eyes blinked. The captain gave instructions to a telephone operator in the back of the room. The snarling Mokhtar was led away. An image of the Sahraoui holding the pistol in his face raced through Marc's mind. He had no regrets for him. Still, Mokhtar had brought them through the desert. Marc would pass a word on to the CIA chief which might help him out of jail. All in all, Mokhtar would make a good soldier in the Royal Armed Forces.

It was almost noon before someone in the *Cabinet Royal* had been reached. It was regrettable, the *gendarme* who had been battling with the telephone informed them. It seemed that the office of the Director of the Cabinet of the Aides of His Majesty Hassan II of Morocco was closed. Marc groaned at the flossy title. Everyone was quite aware of Dlimi's role as Morocco's strong man, Number Two in the realm. More like Chief Thug Not to be Disagreed With. It was suggested that they call back next week, when Colonel-Major Ahmed Dlimi would surely be there.

Marc leaned over the captain's desk once more. "I would like to suggest contacting Colonel Dlimi in his home. My information concerning the Polisario leadership and their base camp could be of importance to His Majesty himself. Not only the Royal Palace, but also the American Embassy, will be grateful to you personally if you place me in touch with Colonel Dlimi."

Marc lingered on the last sentence.

For the first time, the captain smiled. In the corner of the room the *gendarme* placed another call. At this time, it seemed the Royal Cabinet was not prepared to give home telephone numbers.

The small room was stifling. Aysha, exhausted, slumped on the hard wood bench. Marc asked a soldier if they could have some food, and shortly a neat stack of steaming brochettes appeared.

It was two p.m. before the message came that Colonel Dlimi was indeed informed of the American's presence in southern Morocco. He should be permitted to get in touch with his embassy. The captain's heavy-lidded eyes popped open. Then the turtle beak puckered in a scowl. A reprimand! He should have telephoned at once.

Marc was permitted to call the American Embassy.

It took half an hour to reach the CIA chief's office in Rabat. Gratefully, Marc heard the cheerful lilt of Dirk McGonigal's secretary.

"We're glad to know you're all right. Dirk is on a Moroccan army plane heading for Agadir," she said. A garbled call had come in from Assa. It sounded as though Marc was being held for ransom. The Moroccans were being most cooperative. Colonel Dlimi had arranged for transport at once, and McGonigal would be flown by helicopter from Agadir to Assa.

Marc replaced the receiver with a grin. When Mokhtar's call was received in the ambassador's office, all hell must have broken loose!

At that moment, two officers in the gray uniform of the *Gendarmerie* arrived to take Aysha to a clinic where her arm would be attended to. Marc prayed that the medical facilities of Assa were more extensive than those of the Polisario camp. Then he winced. The limitless expanse of their desert world was fading; the real world was closing in on them.

He felt a nudge. A breathless young man in a striped *djellaba* announced himself as an emissary from the Pasha of Assa. He had pushed his way through the curious throng massed at the door of the building. The pasha had invited Marc to rest at his quarters until the American authorities arrived.

Marc smiled ruefully. The sudden display of hospitality merely indicated a more sophisticated form of detention. But house arrest would be a luxury—a damn sight better than being shot at and knifed in the back! He hoped the Moroccans wouldn't ask too many questions. Since, in CIA parlance, the American agency was "in bed with the Moroccans," he was better off being taken for a spy than a meddling newspaperman. An independent reporter nosing around in the Sahara was as welcome as a loose canon in the eyes of King Hassan. It would only be a matter of time until they traced his press credentials through the Ministry of Information.

But he could have problems with Dirk McGonigal, too. After all, his agent, Hassan Saadaoui, had been found murdered in Marc's bed, and Marc had not only visited the Polisario camp with a female Polisario spy, he had killed a Sahraoui. He had clearly violated official policy barring Americans from the disputed territory. Furthermore, he had clearly overstepped the parameters of his CIA job, which was merely to pass on a message.

But meanwhile, he had what he wanted—one hell of a scoop for the outside world—and he was in one hell of a hurry to get to an unmonitored telephone or telex machine. Obviously, Assa would provide neither. His colleagues at the wire service undoubtedly thought that he had taken an unscheduled vacation in lotus land.

Chapter Fourteen

At four o'clock Dirk McGonigal arrived in Assa by Moroccan army helicopter. Striding in front of the CIA chief as they entered the pasha's headquarters was a superbly groomed officer. His uniform fit with glovelike snugness; the brassware was new and shiny. Colonel Benlafkih's services had apparently been commandeered by Morocco's security chief to plumb the mystery of the American, already identified as a journalist, who had crossed the Saharan war zone from Algeria in a Polisario Jeep, accompanied by a beautiful Moroccan woman. Surveying the two captives in guerilla garb, the officer wore the curious squint of a banker who has just uncovered a time bomb attached to the main safe. The last thing the Moroccans wanted was an American newsman waxing friendly with the Polisario.

"And so you moved in and out of the enemy camp in their own vehicles?" Colonel Benlafkih's enraged frown demanded every detail. He glanced first at Marc and then at Aysha, now looking gloriously valiant with her arm in a new sling.

"One moment, if you please!" The leonine head of Dirk McGonigal moved between them. " I believe Colonel Dlimi has informed the Royal Armed Forces of our agreement concerning this gentleman. I will therefore speak with Mr. Lamont alone." It was an order.

Colonel Benlafkih blanched. The word of Dlimi, Morocco's strong man, was irrefutable. McGonigal had received the green light. His face a mask of stone, the colonel waved the Americans toward the adjacent room.

"Then I shall speak with *Mademoiselle* Larosien. I am sure that she has nothing to hide from His Majesty's royal service!" he said. Marc winced. Irritated by Dirk's curt refusal to permit even a token debriefing, the Moroccan colonel would use any means to make Aysha talk. Her liaison with the Polisario was tantamount to treason. Marc cursed McGonigal's heavy-handedness. Didn't the old war horse know anything about Arab pride? The CIA was a bunch of callous Neanderthals.

Dirk led the way to the next room and closed the door behind Marc. A devilish smile burst from beneath the shaggy brows as he grasped Marc's hand.

"If you don't look like the Cheshire Cat! May I offer congratulations?"

"Dirk, Hassan Saadaoui is dead!" Marc blurted.

"I know about that. And I'm damned sorry. He was a good man, one of our best. The French filled us in on it. But you've done a hell of a job! The first American to penetrate the guerilla camp! A real breakthrough and an invaluable experience.

"Look, I want to hear the whole story, but first of all, I have to extricate you from the mess you're in right here. The Moroccans don't like it." He hesitated. "Your complete debriefing—and I'm sorry, but I have to insist on that—will have to wait until we get to the embassy 'Bubble.' We urgently need this report. And believe me, you'll owe it to me by the time I get you out of here. You file whatever you want to the wire service when we're through.

"In the meantime," Dirk's fingers closed on Marc's arm, "you are not required to give anything of substance—and I mean *anything*—to the Moroccans."

Marc paused, further irritated by McGonigal's patronizing attitude. What the hell did he owe the CIA? He'd done the required job, even risked his life. Everything else he'd managed on his own with no help from 'The Company,' from getting Aysha's cooperation to going along to Algeria with a murderous bunch of thugs. This was his own account of the Saharan War and nobody else's. He intended to capitalize on it.

Then he softened, remembering the bind he was in at the present moment. How was he going to get Aysha out of the Moroccans' clutches without McGonigal's help? *Oh, hell, roll out the flag,* he thought. *After all, I owe my country something. And in this case, I presume, it only means a few hours' delay in getting my copy out.*

"O.K., I'll go along with it—as long as whatever I say remains undisclosed. Nothing is to get out on this until my series is published. Otherwise I might feel obligated to write about the unfortunate fate of local agents recruited by the CIA, like Hassan Saadaoui," he said evenly.

"No threats, please." McGonigal frowned. Obviously, the chief didn't like being shoved in a corner. "Agreed," he said finally. "We'll double your fee for your trouble."

Answering McGonigal's questions, Marc ran over key points: the camp aswarm with refugees, the presence of foreign advisors, the use of advanced Soviet weapons—above all, the Stalin Organ and the SAM 9 missiles, equipment that mightily exceeded the operational capability of the Bedouin.

"Interestingly, the Polisario apparently have no interest in trying to topple the king at this time. For the moment he serves their purposes," Marc added. "But I do have a problem: I'm concerned about the agent who brought me in contact with them. The Moroccans might get rough with her."

"Do you mean to tell me that the girl who came in with you now was your contact in Marrakech?" McGonigal's guffaw turned into a low growl.

"Look, this game necessarily involved personal relationships, but playing with a Moroccan woman is dynamite. Anyone who had read his primer on the Arab world knows that. You're goddamn lucky you haven't already been dumped in a plastic bag with your throat slit." McGonigal glanced at the ceiling with a wry smile. "We're going to have to dream up a convincing story to pass along to the boss." Marc got the point. McGonigal would go over Dlimi's head— to the King.

"As for this level here, a little *baksheesh* might take care of the problem."

"You think Benlafkih can be bought?" Marc asked.

"Christ! Army officers aren't paid to dress like that," Dirk snorted.

"Let me clear one point. Aysha *was* an agent of the Polisario. She'a a bona fide defector." This was thorny as hell, but Marc was bound to do all he could for her.

"How can a Moroccan be a defector from their enemy? The Moroccans won't see it that way," McGonigal retorted, his scruffy brows angling into exclamation points.

There was another problem, too. Marc trod softly, remembering Dirk's ban on guns. His brief narration of the killing of Oufkir carefully omitted Aysha's role.

Dirk's head swiveled fiercely, as though microscopic "bugs" might be lurking behind the browning photograph of the darkly handsome king. He gave Marc a hard look.

"Oufkir's track record is well known. The French have evidence he killed Hassan Saadaoui. Forget it! It was self-defense. As far as we're concerned, he disappeared. That's all. Don't bring it up!

"I hope that's your last surprise," he added. "I may run out of cover-ups."

So much for Oufkir!

"By the way, your report might not have the impact you expect. In Washington, attitudes seem to be shifting. There's a changing alignment regarding North Africa." While Marc pondered the significance of that statement, Dirk moved on to further developments.

Meanwhile, popular support of the war in Morocco was dropping, especially as it looked as though it might drag on interminably. So the king had ordered a program designed to alleviate hardship at the front. Soldiers in the war zone were now eligible for double pay and widow's compensation. For the first time, it was announced that troops would be rotated in and out of the desert. These measure would go a long way to boost morale and mitigate against a possible *coup d'etat.*

Marc nodded. The Moroccan monarch knew how to stay in the

saddle, even if it meant introducing a modicum of democracy. McGonigal's source was obviously the horse's mouth. Few foreigners were granted as many private meetings as he was able to enjoy with with Hassan II.

Marc returned to the reception room and sat down beside Aysha on one of the brightly-patterned low divans that lined the walls.

"Was he hard on you?" he asked in a low voice.

"Don't worry about me. I've convinced the good colonel that I was of invaluable help to you."

Suddenly it flashed on him that she was off on a new tack. Of course! She had bowled over the sleek Colonel Benlafkih. They were all putty in her hands. Then he understood something else.

"Oh, God!" he groaned. "Am I right in assuming that you're going to be working for the Moroccans now?"

The slight flutter of eyelids indicated what might be interpreted as assent. Aysha had crossed over to the other side!

Marc turned on her. "Hey, come on! Where's your vaunted idealism? How do you reconcile yourself to a despotic government you claim to despise? This about-face is a bit hard to swallow!"

Aysha blazed back. "Then you understand nothing. I would never betray my country, no matter what the regime!"

She controlled her emotion with an effort. "Don't you know that jailing young people doesn't alter their beliefs, in Morocco or in any other country? Ask Amnesty International! It's the leaders who have to change course."

In Morocco, she claimed, change was inevitable. Reform would have to come one day, or revolution would bring an end to the monarchy. Astute as the king was, he couldn't escape the twentieth century. The population would double by the end of the century, and the next generation would be even more difficult to suppress. There would be that many more non-elites to deal with.

Marc collapsed against the pillows. His peal of laughter released a host of emotions.

"Do the Moroccans know that the balance of forces has tilted their way? Do they have any idea of what they're getting?" he joshed.

Oh, Aysha! She was capable of anything. Romantic, impulsive, headstrong, yet always adapting. Aysha was a survivor.

The door opened, and a large olive-complexioned man in a green uniform entered the room. Behind him padded the hefty McGonigal. He had been about his business, straightening out the details, smoothing away wrinkles that could entangle Marc in the web of Moroccan bureaucracy that led to expulsion or jail.

The Pasha of Assa greeted Marc cordially, apologizing for the delay. Now he wished to invite his guests to dine with him on the best *couscous* in Morocco.

Yes, thought Marc, *the pasha's been busy all right, getting the word from McGonigal.* He took his place with the others seated on the floor around a table of chiseled brass, observing the elongated arabesque of Aysha's arm as she lifted a glass of orange juice.

It came to him that she incarnated the spirit of a changing world. Young people like her in developing nations were sounding the very same note that Americans and Europeans had struck decades before. At last, they were demanding for their peoples the freedom of speech and movement that industrialized countries now took for granted. Perhaps Aysha and others who sought change were learning, as Ghandi taught, that the less violent path served them better. After her experience among the Polisario, she would convince others.

His thoughts were cut short by the sight of a steaming pyramid of *couscous* borne shoulder-high by a young soldier. He had forgotten how ravenous he was. Through the window he saw the green star on a red field, the Moroccan flag, flying straight in the strong, hot wind of the desert, and he was grateful to be where he was.

At sundown the Chinook helicopter rose on a cushion of dust, spewing sand in all directions. It veered away from the patch of open desert that served as an airstrip, then seesawed rakishly in playful updrafts as the pilot sought the protection of steep, tree-covered mountains. It was Polisario-prone territory, and the large aircraft made an easy target. Through the gaping rear vent, Marc followed the amorphous lines of a mobile abstraction. Hazy colors and shapes swirled in the churning air, mingled and confused like his memories of the past few days.

The desert fell away. Above it, wispy patches of mist glowed pink, reflecting the brilliant fireball slipping under its rim. Far behind was the curling wave of the Ouarkziz. Beneath him, small peaks formed a loose pattern of green scrub on brown, uninterrupted by roads. Here and there, a path indicated the way to a small village in the sparsely-populated region. These rocky grottos, ravines and cliffs formed a patchwork of natural hideaways, where it was far easier to conceal oneself than in the open desert. It was not surprising that the Polisario frequently hid within the borders of Morocco to stage their attacks. He had the feeling that his reporting of the war was just beginning.

Near the outskirts of the town of Goulimine, the helicopter turned north to pass over the Anti-Atlas range and fly on to Agadir. Hunched in a corner, Marc Lamont was scribbling notes, the outline of a series of articles that would tell the story of the war in the Sahara on the other side of the ocean. He paused for a moment, realizing that he had not asked Dirk McGonigal what he meant by "shifting attitudes" toward Morocco in Washington.

Chapter Fifteen

"If you don't mind, Mr. Lamont, I'd like you to go over once more exactly what military hardware you saw at the edge of the Polisario camp...that is, before you joined the defecting Sahraoui and the woman in the Jeep."

The ill-humored sarcasm hung suspended in the motionless air of "The Bubble." Army Colonel Norman Baskell had fired the first salvo at Marc Lamont's debriefing in the American Embassy. A well-known Arabist with thirty years in the service, the owl-faced Baskell was fluent in Moroccan and several other Arab dialects. It was part of the deal Marc had made with Dirk McGonigal in Assa that the ambassador and key State Department and military officers would be present, and Marc found himself in the unusual position of defending what he said he saw.

When I interviewed them a week ago, Baskell and his colleagues barely gave me the time of day, Marc mused. *It didn't occur to them that I would end up in the Polisario camp. Now any one of these colonels would enjoy making a barbecued mechoui of my carcass. If one of them had had the opportunity to look at the rebel's operation, his military promotion would be assured.*

Once more, Marc described the oddly-shaped tubes of the Stalin Organ and the pyramids of SAM missiles. Sharp-toothed questions tore at the details.

"*About* a thousand missiles? Can't we be more specific, Lamont?"
"You mean you didn't actually *see* any East German advisors?" And the like. In front of Marc lay several pages of notes written the evening

before on the helicopter flight to Agadir and on the Moroccan C-130, in which he had flown on to Rabat. He had already had enough of the third degree and was champing the bit to file his report to Global Wire Service in Paris.

It had seemed quite routine that morning when he stepped into the strange chamber that staffers called "The Bubble," an oblong plastic box that was raised a few inches off the floor and almost filled a large room. The transparent walls were designed to defy bugging (though the Soviets once got around that by planting a bugging device into somebody's shoe). Today it was his solo show.

At nine a.m., the nabobs of the embassy had already gathered around the oval table. Presiding was Ambassador Henry Vogel, his round face creased in a kindly smile. Next to the ambassador was his priggish deputy, Peter Mastin. Then came the long-faced political counselor. Burly Dirk McGonigal and two young CIA case officers were next. The military team was lined up across from them, led by stiff-lipped Norm Baskell for the Department of Defense. Steve Zasada and Kevin Malone, colonels in the Army and Air Force, were rustling papers like salivating dogs. A bewildered-looking fellow who had just arrived in Rabat represented the Navy's waning interest in Morocco.

Sitting at the ambassador's right was a large, dark-haired man whom Marc had never met and who was introduced as Stan Arikos. President Carter had recently appointed him Special Assistant on Sahelian Affairs in the State Department.

Expressions on the circle of faces ranged from chagrined to bristling, depending on the man's character and job—for Marc had had an experience any one of them would give his eye teeth for. U.S. policy, strange and nonsensical as it was, had been clearly stated: no government official was permitted to enter the Western Sahara, as long as it remained a disputed territory. Meanwhile, an utterly unknown greenhorn, a lowly wire service reporter, had sneaked into the area and toured the Polisario main camp in Algeria, ostensibly as a captive. Now they were going to rip his story apart.

Repeatedly, Colonel Baskell returned to one subject. It was

obvious that Aysha had played a major role in every aspect of the trip. Baskell scratched at details that might reveal a romantic involvement. The young CIA types exchanged gleeful leers, while the other military officers maintained a stony façade. Baskell presumed it had been impressed upon Marc that whatever he had seen and heard in the Polisario camp was critical intelligence not to be shared with a double agent whose allegiances were flagrantly open to question.

"For Christ's sake, it was Miss Larosien who put me in contact with these people!" Marc exploded.

They're jealous, he thought. *Just like a clique of schoolboys. I've trespassed into their magic circle.*

"You seem to slight the guerilla operation," Peter Mastin observed. "Haven't you forgotten that these Sahraoui are fighting for the right to decide their own future?"

"Three-quarters of the camp population are not from the Spanish Sahara!" Marc barked. "They're refugees and mercenaries from the Sahel, lured with promises of food and jobs which, by the way, are paid for by the Red Cross and Algeria."

"We have good relations with Algeria. Why rock the boat?" the political counselor put in cautiously.

"The fact that the U.S. buys gas and oil from Algeria shouldn't color our thinking. It's about time the truth came out," Marc said in a tired voice.

He was jolted by the negative reaction. He had imagined quite a different welcome. He had expected these people would have been all ears. These ears appeared to be deaf. He noted that the visiting State Department VIP Arikos had not spoken during the debriefing. He had listened intently and taken notes.

Marc felt that what he had said was fairly clear: an effort was being made to set up a phony state in the Sahara, propped up by Soviet arms and supported by Morocco's oil-rich neighbors, Algeria and Libya. The very existence of Morocco, a long-time U.S. ally whose limp economy relied on phosphate exports, was jeopardized. In this cool reception, something more than jealousy was involved.

After the meeting, Marc followed the ambassador to his spacious office. They were acquainted from Vogel's previous posts in India and Pakistan. The gray-haired diplomat was a foot shorter than Marc, but he compensated for his size with a quiet dynamism that impressed one at once. He took the time to sound out other people's views. As an ambassador he was unusual in that he liked to discuss issues with reporters.

"So you got back unscathed. Quite a coup!" Henry Vogel closed the door to his office.

Marc shook his head. He hadn't had that impression from the other comments he'd heard.

"Don't pay any attention to the disenchanted brass. The disgruntled colonels were out for blood. Envy probably!" A shadow passed over Vogel's face. "But there have been some changes in American thinking on the Western Sahara. Stan Arikos, the new Special Assistant for Sahelian Affairs, gave us quite a briefing the other day. His area is the drought-stricken region south of Morocco, of course, but he has decided views on the Saharan question. Rather negative, I'm afraid, from the Moroccan point of view.

"Actually though, I guess I haven't told you the other news. I'm going back myself at the end of the month. For good," Henry Vogel said blandly.

Marc jumped. The ambassador leaving? Reputedly, he was the core of the U.S. mission in Morocco. Without him, the military CIA and State personnel would be at each other's throats. Only the deepening lines at the corners of his mouth revealed the tension Vogel was suffering.

The ambassador continued almost casually. He hadn't been officially informed of his impending departure yet, but he had learned in a roundabout way that President Carter had appointed State Department spokesman James Hoskins to his post. He wasn't happy about it, of course, but he'd find something to do back in Washington. Hell, everybody liked to stay on in Morocco. It was the best post in Africa!

"My way of handling things seems to have gone out of style," he added. The light note was forced, and Marc was not fooled.

In Washington, the ambassador continued, the tide seemed to be turning against an old ally. Even in State, Morocco was out of favor. There were important commercial factors to be considered, it seemed. In any event, Marc's reports constituted a major contribution that would shed light on the true state of affairs in the Sahara.

Marc left the ambassador's office, his head reeling. Why was Vogel being sacked virtually overnight—even before he'd been officially informed? He was the best man they'd had in Morocco in years. He had the king's ear, and Hassan II could be a hard man to deal with. In fact, he was closer to the king than any American ambassador had been in decades. Vogel was also a supporter of the Moroccan cause in the Sahara.

In the hall downstairs he stopped short. Someone he hadn't expected to see was flashing his press card at the guard. Tony Joka, a fledgling reporter from New York, had been trying for months to get some sort of assignment out of Paris. With a pencil wedged behind the ear, he epitomized the Joe College look. Now Tony Joka was in a hurry. Marc almost got by him when Tony recognized him.

"Hey, Marc, I got my battle story! I just got back from a press conference in Algiers—via Paris, of course. Can't get there from here, ya know. The border's closed. Those Polisario guerillas are great guys! They gave me an exclusive on how they control the desert. The military attachés upstairs want me to brief them on Polisario victories."

"Maybe Algeria's not your best source, man. I mean it's not their war. Why don't you check your statistics with the Moroccans?" Marc remarked wryly.

"Hell, that's war, isn't it? Death tolls are always inflated. The Moroccans would only give me a reverse count."

Marc laughed. "Well, you may not be far off there, but you ought to check anyway. Did you see any Cubans?" In the camp, Raimondo Gonzalez had mentioned that they were setting up a system of communiqués for the Polisario out of Algiers.

"I don't know, don't think so! Are you trying to put me on?"

Tony gave Marc a sidelong glance.

"Can you tell the difference between a Sahraoui and an Algerian, and for that matter, between an Algerian and a Cuban?"

Joka threw him an impatient look and stepped up to the grill at the bottom of the stairs, where the secretary who would escort him up was waiting.

Marc scowled. More propaganda, more twisting of facts. All over Africa, civil wars and border conflicts were spewing out figures to a gullible world press, which couldn't afford to keep correspondents on the spot. Even when the reports were accurate, they shed little light on what forces were at work below the surface. It took many visits and a lot of time to figure out what was really going on. For an "outsider," it was impossible to know where truth lurked. Tony was definitely an "outsider."

Marc hadn't bothered to tell Tony that he had visited the Polisario lair. Tony had a lot to learn—and he would, the hard way, by making colossal mistakes. Meanwhile, the rest of the press would be picking up those Algerian statistics. They needed to be discredited convincingly. He had seen a lot of things in the Polisario camp that would contradict the propaganda coming out of Algeria.

Now the desk clerk called over to Marc. Mr. Arikos would like to see him in his office. Arikos, the man who had apparently become a powerhouse in the State Department almost overnight. Well, good, he'd like to get Arikos' viewpoint on the Sahara. Marc mounted the stairs again.

"Stan Arikos!" His hand was seized in a metallic grip. The large man's cordial expression creased into a half-smile, pulling the full lips out of kilter. Marc felt himself bored by dark, enameled eyes. These and his sleekly coiffed black hair contributed to a dashing Hollywood look.

"Marc Lamont, great! I've been wanting to talk to you privately. As you know, I've been given the job of taking care of the starving victims of the drought in the Sahel. We're going to be helping them out with a whopper of a program, one of the biggest aid programs in history. But meanwhile, at the personal request of the president, I'm beginning to look into the Saharan problem."

He settled into a chair and motioned to Marc to do the same.

"I was impressed by your report from the Polisario camp, Marc. You seem to be the one person who's not only been there but is aware that a costly, drawn-out war over possession of the territory is a distinct possibility. You're also a smart newsman, I've been given to understand. So you might as well be in on the latest policy regarding the Sahara, and I mean straight from the White House." Arikos paused. Marc got the point. Arikos' emphasis on the last two words was designed to make his direct line to the top patently clear.

"The United States is not going to be involved in this fracas in any way, one way or the other. We're not going to be supporting either side."

Marc jumped to his fee. "Neither side! The Polisario Front doesn't need any support."

"To be succinct, Morocco's going to go it alone, as far as we're concerned. And that means we won't be selling them any military hardware. You might as well work that into your account right away." Arikos permitted himself to indulge in a smug smile.

"You know the Polisario are using Soviet SAM Missiles and the Stalin Organ, supplied by Libya. Algeria is giving them a free haven, obviously taking advantage of the opportunity to thwart Morocco, topple the monarch and install a pro-Soviet government, without having to do the fighting themselves. Isn't that of concern to the United States?" Marc blurted it out.

"I heard what you said at the briefing. You did a great job. Just get it out to the world now that it's not our business." Arikos busied himself with the papers on his desk. End of interview.

Arikos was obviously not going to get into any kind of discussion. The goddamn S.O.B.! The patronizing bastard! Telling him what to write. Marc put away his steno pad and left the office. Somebody was turning around the tables in Washington, and he wanted to get back there soon.

Chapter Sixteen

At one a.m. Marc Lamont found himself alone in the Washington bureau newsroom of Global Wire Service. It was about time for the early-morning reports out of Beirut. *At what exact moment does the day's slaughter begin?* he asked himself. *How much of a journalist's life is consumed by waiting for the inevitable to happen?* For the past two months since he'd left Morocco, his time seemed to have been swallowed up by events in the Middle East, and that meant waiting around for the bombs to go off. A macabre occupation! Wasn't there a better way to influence history? To bring about some change for the better, in exchange for the hours spent covering thousands of pages with scribble?

Abruptly two of the telex machines lining the opposite wall burst into neurotic chatter, spewing out paper like anxious tongues. Marc ran a hand through his hair and shook his head drowsily. He got up to monitor the messages.

"Sporadic firing in Beirut." So what's new? "Begin authorizing more Israeli settlements in Arab territory." That's not exactly new either. He yawned wearily. The machinery clattered on, now solo, now in unison, another duet. A cable from the Paris bureau caught his attention. A Polisario communiqué from Algiers had been relayed.

"The town of Smara in the Western Sahara was occupied yesterday by guerilla forces. Five thousand Polisario independence fighters converged on the Moroccan-held town from three directions... "

Five thousand guerillas! Marc whistled sharply through his teeth. The Polisario had stepped up battle strategy. Until now, they had specialized in light guerilla operations, involving two to five vehicles at most. Moving to conventional, large-scale attacks meant a major change in strategy. If the Polisario held Smara, the Moroccan army was in deep trouble. There were only three garrison towns in the Western Sahara. The fall of Smara was crucial. It could be the turning-point in the war. He wondered whether he should try to confirm the story through the French wire service.

But what would this mean for Morocco? More than ever that nation needed permission to buy equipment from the U.S. We should offer some kind of cooperation to counter what Libya and Algeria were getting from the Soviet Union to arm the Polisario. They obviously wanted to surround Morocco and install a pro-Soviet government. Then tribes from the north and south would battle for supremacy, without the leadership of the dynasty that they had known for three centuries—in fact, since the time of Louis XIV.

Memories stirred within him That assignment had meant more to him than any he'd worked on in years. Maybe he'd given it more than it was worth. Reporters tended to get immersed, to allow whatever they were working on to take over their lives. Images surged through his head. Everything that had to do with the desert suddenly appeared amorphous, illusionary, almost as though events in which he'd participated hadn't actually occurred. No one of the individuals he had known there was in reality what he appeared to be. The agent he was sent to find was dead. The French *couturier* was actually in intelligence. The Syrian doctor was a double agent; the renegade Mokhtar, an improbable savior; the freedom-fighter El-Ouali, a tool of Qadhafi; the camel-riding Bedouin, a missile-operator; the Polisario Front, a fraud.

And what about Aysha? The demure translator who turned out to be a spy—who then changed sides! Was she the greatest imposter of them all? Or was it she, with her quaint Berber parable, who had taught him what it was all about? Power plays! The same kind of naked power play he was now seeing in Washington, where truth carried little weight unless there was clout behind it. He knew that somehow he would manage to see Aysha soon. Their lives had become intertwined.

His series on the Sahara, perhaps the best he'd ever written, had run in a few newspapers around the country, on the second page of sections devoted to foreign news. It hadn't exactly caused a sensation. He himself had been brought back from Paris to the wire service's Washington bureau. A demotion? Well, not exactly. Morocco's problems just didn't seem to be on anybody's agenda.

And now he knew why. His present ill-humor could be blamed squarely on the article in front of him. He had gone over every line of the sixteen-page piece in the *Journal of International Relations.* The case against the sale of military equipment to Morocco was presented most thoroughly. The writer sketched the Polisario as a valiant Bedouin corps, fighting for the right to govern themselves. He gave the impression that a band of camel-riders had independently badgered the Moroccan army into a corner, failing to mention that after every battle they scurried to safety in Algeria. No mention of SAM missiles, foreign advisors or Algeria's squadrons of Soviet MiGs. It was nothing but bare-faced lies and omissions.

To redress the balance somewhat, Morocco was currently seeking to purchase U.S. reconnaissance planes and helicopter gunships— exactly what the captive pilot Brahim Najeb had called for. Morocco was an old friend and ally from World War II. Why had this hard-nosed broadside been aimed at a routine U.S. military assistance program paid for by the Moroccans themselves? In view of the Soviet equipment Marc had seen at the Polisario camp, cutting off all military aid was ludicrous.

Strangely, no one seemed to be thinking ahead. There was a policy argument in favor of Morocco, which possessed a highly strategic position at the mouth of the Mediterranean. The American Sixth Fleet's access to that sea was already jeopardized by Qadhafi's finagling in Malta. But nobody seemed to be considering that side of the issue.

What the hell had happened to American foreign policy? To discourage the Soviet-backed plot to destabilize Morocco, only a nudge in the right direction was needed. No troops were necessary, no intervention.

Marc felt his hackles rise. The damnable thing was that the writer of this key article in the prestigious foreign affairs journal was none other than Stan Arikos. Within the past two months, the unassailable Special Assistant for Sahelian Affairs had made a tour of Algeria and the Polisario camps. In fact, he was the only official American who had ever visited the Polisario, thanks to our benighted policy on disputed territories. Rightly or wrongly, this report was considered the last word on the Western Sahara on Capitol Hill. Marc knew from his brief interview with Arikos in Rabat that the policy change had actually taken place when Ambassador Henry Vogel was fired, well before Arikos visited North Africa. There was something fishy about the whole thing. At the bottom of this Marc sniffed a much bigger story than the one he had written, one that might set Washington on its ear.

He decided to make an appointment at the State Department with Stan Arikos the next morning. Why not tackle him head-on? Marc longed to discover what made this operator tick. Why was he so biased on the subject of Morocco? What was his interest in that part of the world? It had come to Marc's ear via a French colleague that Arikos owned a villa on the island of Malta, a very strategic piece of real estate. How did that villa play into the picture?

When Marc was escorted to Arikos' office in the State Department, he found the special assistant reading the communiqué from Algiers.

"Great news! Fantastic! Have you heard about Smara? These guerillas really know how to fight!" The sleek black head turned toward Marc and his face lit up. "Hey! You're the newsman who slipped into the Polisario camp! Great going!"

"Actually I was taken by force into the camp," Marc said. "But it happened that I saw a lot of things they didn't want me to see. Frankly, I don't believe that communiqué."

"Come on, Marc, cool it. You've spent too much time with the Moroccans. You're brain-washed. Listen, everybody in State who backed King Hassan has been replaced. He's become irrelevant, anachronistic. Sit down. Let me give you the story."

Marc let him talk, then posed a few questions. Arikos brushed aside reports of SAM missiles and advanced Soviet arms as highly exaggerated Moroccan propaganda.

"In view of French assertions that Smara was never taken, how can you seriously give credence to that communiqué?" Marc asked, prodding him.

"The French are biased in favor of their former protectorate. Everybody knows that. Listen, I'm sorry, but I've scheduled a call to the president." Stan Arikos stood up and opened the door.

Marc swore under his breath. He had wanted to get around, as subtly as possible, to the villa Arikos had purchased in Malta. Rumor had it it was quite a palace.

Before he left the outer office, he spoke casually to the secretary.

"Miss Simmonds, I'd like to make another appointment with Mr. Arikos, but I understand he's often in Malta these days."

She looked up surprised and smiled, remembering Marc. "He does have a trip scheduled next week," she said noncommittally as she picked up the phone to call the White House.

Three days later, Marc slumped into a chair before a plate-glass window that overlooked the slate-gray waters of the Potomac. Tieless in his crumpled gray slacks and loose jacket, he hardly cut a distinguished figure in the reflection that caught his eye. He wondered if he'd ever make it as Washington bureau chief for the wire service. Did he care? He'd always preferred being in the field and often hankered to get out there again.

But something was changing in him. Perhaps he should settle down in the city, go for the more responsible job. The only element missing in his life here now was somebody to share it with, somebody like Aysha—if he could only find a way to get to her, to sound her out without confronting her head-on. He wasn't very good on the telephone.

He had made a luncheon date with an old friend, a onetime newspaper colleague from his Los Angeles days. Gil Tanner, who was as dapper and well-groomed as Marc was casual, was now employed by the public relations firm hired by Morocco to improve its flagging image in Washington. When Tanner arrived, they immediately launched into a discussion of the subject that interested them most.

"You mean to say the communiqué from Algiers was a blatant lie?" Tanner looked profoundly shocked.

Marc shrugged. That morning he had telephoned Paris to get in touch with a colleague who had covered Morocco's Green March into the Sahara with him. Albert Durix of Agence France Presse was still on the Moroccan beat. In fact, he had been in Smara the day before with a group of diplomats and reporters. It was apparently obvious that the Polisario never took the town. They didn't even get into it, though they had managed to lob in a shell that caused little damage. It had lodged itself rather absurdly in the wall of the town hall where the local *jemaa* met. This was the only evidence to support the fact that the Polisario had been within a few miles of the town before being routed.

"My piece will be in tomorrow's *Post*. But, as you well know, people find the first news of a battle enthralling; they read about it in detail. They never bother with the follow-up denials and retractions. Frankly, reporting on wars is a great way to ensnare the gullible, depending of course on your slant," Marc said.

Gil Tanner nodded. "Nothing like a victory to pad a publicity campaign."

"Right now, it's in style to believe what the Polisario puts out. Poor independence fighters versus a despotic king. Perfect scenario," Marc cut in irritably. In Washington, the man-in-the-know, so to speak, was Stan Arikos. He was the only government official who had touched base all around the Western Sahara, including the Polisario camp. Now that he had written a definitive article in a magazine that functioned as the Bible on foreign affairs, no one would bother to look further. Military assistance to Morocco was doomed.

"You know, this Smara story has turned me on." Marc took a gulp of wine. "Normally I don't give a damn which way politics go, but this thing sticks in my craw."

"Hey! Don't go overboard, Lamont," Gil admonished with a laugh. "If anyone has a reputation for being immune to politics, it's you. I thought the only thing you cared about was accuracy. Seriously, we'd sure like to see some attention paid to an unbiased report like yours. We're not interested in tinkering with the truth, and we don't need to."

"I just thought of something," Marc said thoughtfully. "You know Stan Arikos recently bought a villa in Malta. Six months ago I interviewed two ex-CIA types making a killing in the arms-running trade in Malta. You saw my article on Wilson and Terpil. But with the constant press of news from the Middle East, I haven't gotten back there." Marc was peering intently across the river at a moored lightship painted a gaudy fire-engine red. "I've got a story that's been sitting on the back burner for a couple of weeks that could take me to Malta next week. It has to do with Qadhafi's influence on island politics. Maybe there's a tie-in among some of these things."

Gil raised his wine glass to Marc's. "Lest too light winning... "

"Make the prize light," Marc mumbled, responding to their customary toast. It was one of Gil's literary quotes. He had a passion for Shakespeare.

As Marc drove back to the office, he sifted the facts. What could he possibly accomplish in Malta? Even if he found out something unsavory about Arikos, it wouldn't be easy to reverse current thinking on the Saharan war. Arikos claimed the Polisario were victims of Moroccan imperialism. This anti-Moroccan stance happened to mesh well with the viewpoints of two major Washington lobbies. The U.S. had recently become Algeria's largest trading partner. SONATRACH, the Algerian state firm, had been granted a twenty-year market for natural gas at twice the U.S. price, thanks to some power-pull at the top. In addition, we were importing more than half Algeria's crude oil exports. This unique deal with a Marxist-socialist state swung on well-grounded influence. Former Secretary of Defense Clarence Wells was SONATRACH's man in Washington, and President Carter had just named Wells his "special envoy" to Algiers. If that wasn't inbred, what was?

The powerful Algerian lobby was obviously more geared to financial interests than to truth in politics. But there was further organized opposition to Moroccan aid in the capital. The massive clout of the Jewish lobby was directed against sales of military hardware to any Arab state. Had American Jews forgotten that King Hassan's father, Mohammed V, had saved Moroccan Jews from Nazi gas chambers during World War II?

Didn't they remember that he had named Jews to his cabinet? Weren't they aware that Hassan II had laid the groundwork for the Camp David talks between Jews and Egyptians?

There must be a way to buck these lobbies.

Then a totally brilliant idea sprang into his head. Why not take a few extra days in Malta while working on the Qadhafi story? He would arrange for Aysha to fly over from Morocco. This would fit nicely with her new role, working for Moroccan Intelligence. On the side, he would check out the significance of Arikos' villa. Arikos might even be there.

Most important, he would be seeing Aysha again.

Chapter Seventeen

A dry speck of dust in the Mediterranean, Marc thought as the airplane from Paris approached Luqa airport. Malta's stony topography was barely relieved by clusters of fig, an occasional vineyard and walled terraces girdling precious patches of green. In the distance, a plethora of domes and steeples, beckoning from the capital city, Valletta, gave evidence of the island's medieval history as the southern base of crusading knights. He had noted that the striking mélange of architectural styles added appreciatively to its appeal to sun-seeking tourists, who now formed the major bulwark of the Maltese economy.

The three islands that made up the Republic of Malta were neatly situated mid-point between Gibraltar and Suez, Sicily and North Africa, and their deep harbors also contributed to Malta's desirability as a naval base. Libya's Muammar Qadhafi, intending to make the Libyan fleet a major naval power, was angling for exclusive use of Malta's port. He claimed the U.S. Sixth Fleet was an intruder. In fact, he wanted the naval forces of all nations not bordering on the Mediterranean banned from the sea. Marc's purpose in Malta was to find out how successful Qadhafi's efforts to woo Prime Minister Dom Mintoff had been.

The British, who had used the port as a major base for two centuries, were having their problems, too. Recently, the leftist Mintoff had required the U.K. to triple the subsidy through which they obtained use of port facilities. And so the Brits were gradually leaving. If they pulled out completely as they threatened to, the already-sagging Maltese economy would collapse. The island's inhabitants had been vociferously split on the issue at the time of Marc's last visit.

Meanwhile, the United States was wielding its clout to keep the strategic Grand Harbour open to the Sixth Fleet. And American editors were panting for an exclusive interview with the flinty Mintoff, which as yet Marc had been unable to obtain.

He drove directly to the Hilton on St. Julian's Bay, avoiding the congested capital. It wasn't the most imaginative choice of hotels, but he had appreciated its functioning telephones and telex on his previous trip. Thrown in were the spectacular sea view, three swimming pools and décor recalling the islands' baroque Golden Age.

On his last trip an unexpected encounter with Libyan army officers had paid off. He had run into them at the Casino on Dragonara Point, a favorite watering hole of the North Africans who were denied such pleasures at home. Not wishing to get into a hassle, he had introduced himself as an American business consultant and they had struck up a lively conversation. It turned out that one of the Libyans, Captain Mohammed Al-Kharuubi, had attended college in California.

That evening with the Libyans proved fruitful. Marc had been able to fill in the chinks in his story on the two American arms-runners, Wilson and Terpil, who also frequented Malta. The ex-CIA agents had apparently signed a contract with the Libyans for ten million dollars' worth of illegal munitions. Marc had discovered, too, that the Libyans were now as in favor with the current Maltese regime as the Americans were out of favor. Qadhafi was playing a cat-and-mouse game, offering economic assistance and investment.

At eight o'clock that evening, Marc approached the hotel's reception desk and waited for an opportunity to speak alone with the English night clerk. He had already telephoned Captain Al-Kharuubi and had been invited to join him at a party at a large villa. Marc described the villa's location on a lonely promontory facing St. George's Bay and asked the clerk if he knew to whom it belonged.

"That one, sir. Let me think." The clerk paused. "The owner is

American, yes, definitely an American...no, not Wilson...not Terpil. He has a big job in Washington, sir. Only comes here from time to time, but when he does, he has an awful lot of guests." He smiled obligingly. Marc smiled as well. This might just be somebody he knew!

Half an hour later, Marc drove the car that he had rented along a quaint street of old Valletta overhung with box windows. As he passed under the jutting *miradores*, he felt himself watched by myriad eyes, the same eyes that used to light up when British battleships moved into Grand Harbour. The Floriana Gut, once celebrated for its prostitutes of every nationality, was dismally quiet since relations with Britain had soured.

He passed on to a more residential district where he was to pick up Aysha in a pension. He gave his name to a clerk and sat down, his emotions racing between anxiety and anticipation. Would she be the same? Would they pick up where they had left off? Transatlantic telephone calls revealed so little.

He had told her about the party, and when she appeared, he saw that she had dressed for the occasion. For the first time, he beheld Aysha arrayed in the magnificent framework of imperial Morocco, the centuries-old regalia in which beauty and mystery conspire to create a creature that is at once highly sensual yet somehow distanced and unattainable. Her green satin caftan was cinched at the waist by emerald-studded links of gold, and the same gems shone from her ears and throat. Her dark hair was woven into a regal coiffure piled high upon her head and set in place with a small gold crown. He had never seen her dressed in the customary finery of Fez, the historical capital of a once-grand empire. Under their black lashes, her light topaz eyes astonished him once again. Again they held that confident, almost mocking look that made him immediately aware of how drab life had been without her. Their kiss obliterated time.

"I can't tell you what it means to me that you decided to come," he said, yet he felt that they had never been apart. "You are overwhelming, you know."

"It's the desert emeralds!" she demurred. "An old custom. Arab women wear their riches on their bodies. Thus, if your husband divorces you—as he can, by clapping his hands three times—you take it all with you."

"Well, wherever you're going, you're going with me!" he said.

They sat down together at a little table in the pension's comfortable, old-world salon, and he thought how much better it was to be there than in the vast vacant halls of the hotels he frequented. He explained what had happened. Al-Kharuubi had given him directions to "a friend's villa," where apparently a spectacular party was going on. Everyone of any import on the island had been invited.

"If we're lucky," Marc said, "this will be the right place. I mean it's just possible, if my research is correct, that it belongs to a particular American."

Outside the city he followed the road to the villa on its lonely promontory, guided by Al-Karuubi's directions. At the gate by the road he barely braked, tossing a friendly wave to a guard, who motioned to them to continue down the drive. He inhaled the heady aroma of jasmine pervading the night, already able to hear the sounds of a monumental event. Music blared through long French windows and streams of light beamed out toward St. George's Bay. The "friend's villa" turned out to be a Renaissance palazzo built of Carrara marble and surrounded by lavish gardens. Within, one could see a dozen chandeliers reflected in huge antique mirrors set on red brocade walls.

Only the *nouveau riche* could lay it on like this and invite everyone in town, Marc thought. Nonetheless, getting in might be ticklish. There were two guards in Libyan uniforms at the door, and he didn't want them asking about him inside. As one of the guards moved to speak to him, he let Aysha go ahead. She slipped two Maltese pound notes deftly into the guard's hand, while Marc greeted him amiably in French and wobbled tipsily through the door—the perfect continental gigolo who showed up at all such parties.

Inside, Libyan uniforms mingled with a crowd of well-dressed guests, their elegance enhanced by the sparkling light of the crystal chandeliers. There seemed to be a lot of attractive women, though they were hardly in Aysha's class, he mused. And there in the middle of the room was the host he had hoped to find. He pressed Aysha's hand and melted into a corner.

Aysha knew her cue. She moved directly toward the large man with the sleek black hair, wearing a well-cut business suit. Stan Arikos was playing the genial host, bowing suavely over the hands of female guests. Then his eyes fell on the green caftan, the cleavage, the enticing waist and the bold eyes above it. It was evident that the local tarts, invited for the occasion, were outclassed. Aysha gave him a half smile and murmured a few phrases in French. Arikos was hers.

Abruptly, the sound of shouting from the driveway caught his attention and, as he turned away, he placed a hand on Aysha's shoulder. Gradually, the roar turned into a rhythmic chanting in Arabic. A voice cried, "Long live the leader of the Great Revolution!"

The crowd at the door parted to make way for a thin figure, resplendent in a cream-colored uniform. The lean face was topped by jaunty black curls on which a visored officer's cap perched at a rakish angle. His jaw was creased in the famous victor's grin. The man stopped in the middle of the room, leaned back to receive the ovation and waved clenched fists with mock ferocity.

"Brother Colonel!" a young officer cried out deliriously. All eyes were glued on the charismatic figure of Muammar Qadhafi as he greeted Stan Arikos. The American beamed and they clasped hands warmly. As Qadhafi's dark eyes, piercing and fanatic, bore into Aysha's, she felt their powerful, almost mystical effect.

Marc slipped through the French doors onto the terrace, assured that Aysha could take care of herself. He had never before seen the Libyan leader in the flesh. The meeting between Qadhafi and Arikos was front-page news, but above all, he had to avoid being recognized by Arikos. As for Qadhafi, his humors were notoriously unpredictable. People oceans away received the death sentence at the whim of the dictator, and Marc had no wish to get on that list. He was also avoiding Al-Kharuubi, whom he had seen in the crowd with Arikos. Nonetheless, one way or another, he had to find out what the meeting was about.

He spied a figure watching him from the balustrade by the garden and recognized Lt. Abu Bakr Al Gayed, one of the Libyans he had met previously. They had had a few long talks together, and Marc had discovered that the lieutenant's English was fluent. Al Gayed had been overshadowed before by the garrulous Al-Kharuubi, and now, as Marc sauntered over in a friendly manner, the young man seemed glad of company.

"The girls are a fickle bunch!" Al Gayed said sourly. "My friend attaches herself to the host whenever he's in town. Forgets about me entirely."

"Always going where the money is, right?" Marc said sympathetically and asked about the officer's job in Malta.

Al Gayed chatted willingly. He assisted Al-Kharuubi in keeping track of Libyan interests in Malta. There were a number of programs. For example, "The Leader" was offering the Maltese free immigration into Libya in exchange for the training of Libyans in Malta. On this trip, Brother Colonel was negotiating with the Prime Minister to put an air base on Malta to serve Libya's naval flotilla.

Marc chuckled. The news would kindle fury in the U.S. and Great Britain. His trip was paid for whether he got to see Mintoff or not.

"What does Qadhafi's trip have to do with the American?" he asked.

Al Gayed whistled piercingly. "Haven't you heard of the dream closest to The Leader's heart? A united Sahara!"

Marc nodded. It was well known that Qadhafi had a mystical reverence for the desert. The chief of state disappeared into the wilderness to meditate for months at a time. Born to a family of herdsmen, Qadhafi rated the Bedouin code of asceticism and honor as high as Islam, higher than advanced education. He saw himself assuming Nasser's mantle as the great Arab leader.

"Qadhafi's Saharan state will unite all desert nations in Islamic socialism," Al Gayed explained. "It's an ideological—a religious— cause. The Polisario's SADR is its embryo. That's why Libya is paying the bill for millions of dollars of Soviet military hardware for the Polisario.

"This American shares his enthusiasm," he added. "His special interest is the Sahara."

Marc pondered, frowning. Did Arikos really share Qadhafi's dream of a great Arab socialist state? Qadhafi was a notorious fomenter of terrorism. Even his Arab brothers didn't trust him, and many mergers with other nations that he had attempted to date— with Tunisia, Algeria, Syria, Egypt and Sudan—had all failed. There had to be more to it than that.

"This American is influential. He has assured The Leader that no arms will be sold by the United States to Morocco!" Al Gayed said with a glint in his eye. He had no love for Stan Arikos.

Marc blinked. A guarantee to Qadhafi? The idea was staggering. He asked about Terpil and Wilson.

Al Gayed smiled. The former operatives had successfully delivered a shipment of arms to Libya. Now they were training Libyans in CIA methods. Things were moving according to The Leader's plan.

More hitmen! Marc's mind reeled. *That's all the world needs. And these renegades held their rendezvous in Arikos' villa! But that's another story—or is it?* He turned to look at the throng in the salon, feeling an urge to charge in and confront Arikos with a bald accusation. But even his presence at the party was risky.

In the salon, Aysha felt a twinge of pain. She was involuntarily glued to Arikos. His large paw had closed in a vice-like grip on her arm. She felt his breath, stale and acrid on her cheek, as the combined odor of cigar, cologne and hair tonic engulfed her.

Posing as an available woman, she could hardly object to Arikos' attentions. Relieved, she saw a Libyan officer moving purposefully toward them.

To the other's questioning look, Arikos said gruffly, "We can speak in English, Captain Al-Karuubi. She's North African." Obviously he resented the intrusion.

The Libyan nodded, his eyes traveling appreciatively around the green caftan. "You wanted to see me?"

"I have to talk to you about funds. I'm running low." Arikos' whisper was urgent.

The Libyan looked miffed. "We put the equivalent of a million dollars in your account at the Bank of Malta nine months ago."

"Sure, that covers the price of the villa, but I have maintenance. I need another half million to entertain you people."

"Qadhafi said a few thousand would do."

"Does Qadhafi want arms or not?" Arikos rasped. His fingers closed on Aysha's arm, the manicured nails jabbing painfully, as the other man enumerated the Libyan shopping list in a low whisper.

She caught the words "submachine guns, M40 grenade launchers, a thousand M-16 rifles."

This was it! The Arikos-Qadhafi connection. The Libyan captain was glaring at her pointedly. She gave him a benign blank stare and wrenched her arm loose from Arikos' grasp. She must find Marc. She had to remember the weapons, the numbers. She began to work her way through the crowd. Arikos' heavy tread followed. The vice closed on her arm again, jerking her body backwards. She forced her head in his direction.

"*Plus tard*!" Her smile was pure honey. She only needed two minutes to find Marc.

Arikos refused to be put off.

"*En haut, maintenant!*" He fumbled in French, his eyes rolling toward the ceiling.

Her smile was wearing thin, and she felt herself trembling.

"*Un moment!*" She slipped away to the hall, looking for the powder room, anywhere to escape the odious brute. Where had Marc wandered off to?

Arikos followed. He had her by the waist now. He was forcing her up the stairs, yet she dared not call attention to herself. A shriek stuck in her throat as a horrible vision flashed before her. El Ouali with the whip! Dazedly, she clawed for a grip on the banister. Oh, God, she mustn't faint!

A commotion broke out abruptly in the crowded room below. Somebody screamed, "Where's Arikos? Get a doctor immediately!

Qadhafi!"

The startled Arikos turned back, and Aysha fell limp against the stair.

At that moment on the terrace Marc was taking his leave of Al Gayed. The lieutenant had avenged himself on Arikos, it seemed, but it would be wise to disappear before Al Gayed realized how much information he had leaked.

Just then, a set of French doors farther down the terrace flew open. A lean figure in white burst into the night. Behind him, a security man held the doors, motioning to those behind not to follow. The man on the terrace tore off his visored cap and waved it, as if in a desperate effort to cool himself. With frenzied hands, he tore at his hair, then pulled at his jacket, yanking off buttons. He gasped for air, as though he couldn't breathe, even now in the open air. Stumbling against the balustrade, he fell on his face and lay prostrate on the terrace, his torso heaving like pumped bellows.

Marc watched in fascinated horror. Qadhafi had spells. It was said he took drugs, he had trouble sleeping. The stories about the man were legendary. This was the fit of a madman!

Then he saw Aysha running toward him, her caftan pulled to one side. Her look of horror surprised him.

"Get me out of here!" she gasped.

Behind her through the glass door, he spotted a looming figure watching them. Arikos was trying to force his way by a Libyan security team. No one was permitted to witness the illness of "The Leader."

Marc seized Aysha's hand. Together they ran to the end of the terrace and rounded the villa to where the rented car was parked. With a sob of relief, Aysha lay back against the seat, and the car shot down the road. When they reached the main road, Marc waved cheerily at an armed guard and floored the accelerator.

The man had been alerted. A shot rang out, then another. The car careened to safety around a corner, and Marc headed straight for the airport.

Minutes later, in a secluded lounge, Marc pressed Aysha to him.

"I am so sorry. I never thought he'd try to work so fast," he said, offering her a Scotch.

"Just water, please," she said. She was calm. The color had returned to her face.

"Nothing actually happened, thanks to Qadhafi. It was so close! The brute paralyzed me with fear. I couldn't cry out. But it doesn't matter now. I got what you wanted, Marc!" She beamed her best smile at him.

"Got what?" he said, struck by her change of mood.

"The Arikos connection! Qadhafi put a million dollars in Arikos' account to pay for the villa. He's asking for another half a million for maintenance!"

Marc stared at her. "Are you sure of what you're saying?"

"The Bank of Malta, *mon amour*. The Libyan captain said it." She took another drink from the glass and eyed him triumphantly. Arikos was pulling strings for Libya in Washington. He was a powerful man, wasn't he? From his position he could work wonders for Qadhafi. Captain Al-Kharuubi had listed the weapons he wanted.

"God, what you went through for this! Of course. An agent of influence bought and paid for by Brother Colonel!" Marc scowled. It was the answer to everything. Arikos was on the take. Arikos was blocking Moroccan aid. Arikos had tried to muzzle the press. All they needed now was hard evidence, a letter or the bank statement.

Aysha was aware of a chasm in her stomach. "The only trouble is, he saw us together. He knows I'm with you, and he'll realize I understood it all," she said.

"You'll have to leave on the next plane for Rome," Marc said, all business now. "He doesn't know your name. He probably didn't recognize me in the dark. For now, we won't travel together."

She looked surprised.

He seized her again. "You're not getting away this time, my love. Two months was too long. I've missed you, Aysha, more than I can ever say. This separation has convinced me totally that I want you with me in Washington. You can do whatever you like. I know you're proud as hell, but I think you care for me." He felt sheepish. He wasn't used to courting a woman with words.

She looked at him for a moment in her quizzical way. Then she smiled and said, "Marc, I've been wondering how long it would take you to say something like that. Perhaps I'm not as proud and unattainable as you thought!"

"You have every reason to be proud. I'm proud of you!" he said, brushing her nose with a kiss. Then he placed a rectangular audio cassette on the table. "But I'm not above using you, too. Would you mind taking my preliminary report with you to the Paris bureau? Just in case."

She nodded.

"I'll meet you there tomorrow with your luggage. Give me five minutes."

"*Superchouette*," she said laughing, which translates into something like, "Fantastic!"

Chapter Eighteen

Aysha replaced the receiver and looked from the hall across the living room where Marc was engrossed in the *Washington Post*. Through the window behind him, she could barely see the blue Potomac through the summer foliage. They had been in Washington for two days and already she felt intrigued by the busy city. Its impelling pulse was fascinating to her. Its denizens appeared to be well-traveled, educated people, both foreign and American, and it was the hub of the United States. She liked its great open spaces, its Mall, its museums and parks.

"Damnation!" Marc exclaimed, still reading. "Tony Joka has another piece in on the Western Sahara. This time he got to the Polisario camp. The way he paints the guerilla lifestyle they look like heroic martyrs. He doesn't even mention the Libyan and Algerian roles. You know, anyone would fall for this romantic garbage!"

"*Cherie*, you didn't hear my conversation. I've got an appointment for an interview tomorrow at the National Council on U.S.-Arab Relations. They're considering me for a position dealing with women's affairs," Aysha said with a Cheshire Cat grin. She pirouetted gracefully and planted a kiss on his forehead.

"My God, Aysha, hold it. There's no rush for you to go to work. Suppose that Stan Arikos runs into you one day?" He frowned.

"I don't have the job yet, Marcus Aurelius. I'm just going to talk to them. Did you expect me to sit here reading your articles all day? I can look like somebody else." She whirled around to stare at her image in the hall mirror and twisted her abundant fall of dark hair into a bun.

"So you're going to turn yourself into a Washington power-broker, a feminist predator. Uh-oh! Poor guys!" He smiled. But she was knowledgeable and highly intelligent. The job would be right up her alley. And, he thought, glowing inside, it would keep her busy and happy in Washington.

"Oh, hell. You'll be running the Council in no time!" He laughed.

Just one more reason to get the case against Arikos moving. The arms-for-Morocco issue was coming up before the House Foreign Affairs Committee next week.

First he had to make that important call from the apartment, which was why he had not yet gone to the office. With taut fingers he dialed the State Department number, his mind racing. *Oh, God, let the bastard still be living it up in Malta!*

"I'm sorry. Mr. Arikos is out of town!" The voice was crisp.

Good news! Pat Simmonds, the secretary, was in. Arikos was still out. While the cat's away, the mouse would play. He remembered her friendly manner. How much did she know, he wondered. How much did Arikos confide in her? Probably not much. She was impressionable and talkative. Possibly she wasn't aware of any improprieties.

"Sorry to miss him. I'm afraid I'm in rather of a hurry for some vital information. Could we meet for lunch?" he asked boldly. "No? Look, this is urgent. A lot of things could be hanging in the balance for your boss, which should be of some concern to you, too. How about a drink this evening?"

It took persuasion. Like everyone else in Washington, she was leery of the press, but she was curious. He had to see her before Arikos returned from Malta. Evidently, he had said just enough.

Marc replaced the receiver and caught his own image in the mirror—the unruly, sandy-colored hair, the long, lean face. Not exactly a Lothario.

"Well, Aysha, what are the odds? Will she tell me anything?" he asked.

"Possibly. In spite of your saturnine look and your infatuation with your own toughness, Marc, you do have a certain Yankee charm!" she replied teasingly.

"Thanks for the flattery. I'm from California," he parried.

She took his hands in hers and looked into his eyes. "You're a little bit of everything, Marc. That's why I love you and that's why I'm going to stay here with you."

This time she was speaking from the heart. A great wave of calm engulfed him, for he knew that his future was now bound to hers and that that was what he most wanted.

The choice of locale was important. Nothing too showy, nor too crowded where conversation would be overheard. He decided on the penthouse bar at the top of the Marriott in Rosslyn. Outside the city, Pat Simmonds was less likely to run into someone she knew.

His news analysis of the Saharan situation had been published that day. He had refuted every point in Arikos's article in the *Journal of International Relations* without reference to the piece. It hadn't been easy, for Arikos had twisted the facts to present an air-tight argument against selling military equipment to Morocco. State Department, CIA and most of Congress, goaded by the Algerian and Jewish lobbies, had come to agree with Arikos' stand.

So if Marc was going to see this thing through, there were two power blocks in Washington to take on as well as Arikos, those seemingly amorphous, but tightly controlled brokers of influence. To start with the Jewish lobby, he had had real luck in nailing down a luncheon date with Senator Sol Rosen of New York for the next day. Rosen was a one-man institution whose influence reached far beyond the Senate. Single-handedly, if he cared to, he could turn around the Jewish vote. Their only real gripe against Morocco was that it was Arab. Any Arab nation appeared as a threat, but they hadn't really looked at the facts concerning Morocco. Getting Rosen to say or do anything of significance was the problem. Marc would have to rely on his powers of persuasion, as well as his writing.

Blocking the Algerian lobby wouldn't be so difficult once he had exposed Arikos. And for that, of course, he needed proof of corruption, of the funds furnished to Arikos by the Libyans, and that was what he was going after now. He smiled. For the first time, he was moving beyond the parameters of his routine reportorial chores.

It was a clear evening. From the top of the Marriott, the lighted monuments made a vivid panorama—the Cathedral looming on the hill, Georgetown University ramparts across the Potomac and, far to the right, the dome of the Capitol. Washington was Marc's favorite city, after Paris.

Pat Simmonds scanned his face warily. While they waited for their order, he ranged over a number of subjects, flattering her intelligence, he hoped. She seemed to be waiting for him to come to the point, but terrified to mention it. After a cocktail, he suggested dinner. It wasn't until they were finishing dessert and her coolness had thawed that he mentioned the villa on Malta.

Her forehead furrowed. "How did you hear about that? Mr. Arikos rarely talks about his private life."

Marc ignored the query. He was building his scenario.

"Perhaps it's not so private. There is some question as to how your boss could afford such a sumptuous palace. I don't want to alarm you, but there are people whose job they think it is to look for corruption in government, even in the most innocent of situations. Certain talk has come to my attention—and well, I thought perhaps I should warn you." Now he was tiptoeing, gently twisting her arm.

She looked distressed, but controlled. His eyes traveled around the dining room. It was almost empty now.

"I can't mention names. I can only say that questions are being asked on two scores. First, people want to know what Mr. Arikos' connections with the Libyans is, and secondly, how he obtained the funds to buy and maintain the villa. Obviously, he couldn't do it on his salary at State. In other words, your boss may be involved in some unsavory business that could blow into a major scandal."

She appeared stunned by the last sentence.

He leaned closer. "Pat, you're an attractive, capable woman. You can work for anybody."

Arikos' secretary fumbled nervously with her napkin. Her mouth remained firmly shut, but a barely noticeable tic at its corner made him think he was making progress.

"Undoubtedly, you wish to keep your own name clear. If you cooperate, I think we can avoid bringing you into it, even after my story breaks in the newspapers—and let me assure you it will!" He hoped he was getting through to her.

Pat Simmonds gasped. "You mean I could be dragged into it?"

"Yes, as a knowing accessory, harboring information." It was the truth, more or less.

"What do you need?" she asked softly.

"Do you know if Arikos has made regular deposits into a special account? Perhaps here, more likely abroad."

Pat was scared now, her face chalky white. She balked.

"I can't do it," she said flatly.

"We know that Mr. Arikos uses this villa in ways that are detrimental to U.S. interests. All of that is going to come out."

He thought she might collapse, and for a moment he pitied her.

"Yes." She barely breathed the word. Obviously she knew more than she had let on. "There is a record of deposits made to a Maltese bank that Mr. Arikos keeps in a special file."

"Can you get it for me?" His eyes were riveted on hers as he leaned forward to catch her words.

She hesitated. Her eyelids fluttered momentarily, like trapped butterflies. "Yes, but it will be hard to trace the funds. The money Mr. Arikos doesn't spend for his vacations in Malta is funneled away to another account. In Switzerland, I think. I don't know where he keeps that file." She slumped back in her chair.

"It's okay. Records of the Maltese account are all we need. Once the ball starts rolling, the rest will come out on its own." He placed a reassuring hand on the one that gripped the table.

"I'll have copies of the account for you tomorrow." She looked out the window, her eyes unseeing, brimming with misery.

"Not in the office," he said. "I'll meet you during your lunch break in the café on Twenty-second Street."

A fleeting thought of sympathy for the turmoil she was

experiencing was obliterated by his own sense of wild elation. He fetched her coat and drove her home.

When he met Pat Simmonds at the café the next day, she was breathless. Her face had a deathly pallor.

"I'm afraid of what's going to happen. Arikos is back in town!" she stammered. Nonetheless, she handed him an envelope.

"Actually you are doing the right thing. In fact, a heroic thing. It's not going to touch you, I promise," Marc said.

With trembling fingers, he checked the contents of the envelope: Xeroxed copies of several pages of the Maltese deposits. It was everything he needed.

"Look, if anything happens and you need help, get in touch with me right away." He touched her arm reassuringly. He was quite aware that he had put her through hell.

As he stepped into the street, he glanced at his watch. His luncheon with Sol Rosen in the Senate dining room was arranged for one o'clock. He couldn't miss that, despite the urgency of getting the proof of Arikos' corruption safely to Global Wire Service. He hailed a taxi going in the direction of Capitol Hill.

Why was he doing all this, he wondered as he settled into the backseat. Why was he putting himself on the line and this poor young woman through the wringer? Why was he stepping out of the role he cherished as the hard-boiled newsman who looked at all sides of every question and never selected one as his own? Did he really care that much about the fate of Morocco or that of a bunch of guerillas in the desert? Or even of the Sixth Fleet in the Mediterranean? He'd be off on a dozen other assignments in the near future. His job was to report the facts, not to manipulate them.

The question that bothered him was whether his feeling for Aysha was pushing him to this. No, he thought, actually it wasn't Aysha, although she was a part of it. The injustice and the lies simply went against the grain. It stuck in his craw that the foreign policy of the United States could be blinded and bent out of shape through the venality of one traitorous public servant. Morocco's case was just one foreign situation in many where the United States could and should show its clout. Perhaps it was of no importance to most Americans, but we had a certain obligation to fulfill to loyal allies. Shouldn't the morality of it outweigh our commercial interests? He grinned. Besides, he could never look Aysha in the eyes again if he didn't go through with it! If he had become *engagé*, a writer who cares about man's destiny, Aysha had had much to do with it.

Senator Rosen was a one-man whirlwind, the center of a swirling vortex of influence, prestige and pressure where it counted. Marc found him talking to three other people at a small table in the congested dining room of the New Senate Office Building. Rosen's assistant was taking notes concerning architectural changes in an apartment complex of which the senator was part owner. The other two men were variously involved in the same financial scheme. *The Capitol Hill Gold Coast working overtime*, thought Marc. He was relieved when the others moved off and he was left alone with the senator.

"We're to be joined by a third party. Hope you won't mind," Rosen said amiably, his polite little eyes darting about the room.

No one around Rosen ever had time to object. There was too much going on. Marc knew that he had been fortunate to arrange any meeting at all. All he wanted was a few minutes of the titan's time to press home a few points. Rosen's answers on their own would make a good piece.

The gray head swiveled toward him now. "Okay. You've got five minutes. Shoot!" Rosen turned to order a sandwich from the waiter standing next to him.

Reaching back into history, Marc hit salient points crucial to Jewish interests in Morocco. Were the senator's constituents aware that Moroccan Jews, although threatened by the Nazis, had not been forced to leave the country, as they had in France? Did they know that it was the personal intervention of the Moroccan king that kept them from concentration camps? And so forth. Finally, he asked whether Senator Rosen personally thought it was in the interest of American Jews to thwart military assistance to Morocco? What was his attitude toward Libyan arms supplied to the Polisario?

The senator had read Marc's article of the day before, and now his remarks were canny and noncommittal. Nonetheless, they would make news. Marc knew that he had scored a few points. He was about to put his tape recorder into his briefcase when the third man appeared. His heart fell into his shoes. It couldn't be, but it was. The slick black hair, the oily manner that reeked of false cordiality.

Stan Arikos' big palm clasped the senator's small white hand. One would have thought he hadn't seen Sol Rosen in ten years. He knew how to lay it on. The nod that acknowledged Marc's presence was noticeably less enthusiastic. Did Arikos know that Marc had been onto his secretary? The papers that could incriminate Arikos were in the briefcase at Marc's feet.

"I don't know what this guy is trying to promote with you, Sol. He has a bug about Morocco." Arikos's opener was suave.

"Marc Lamont seems to have spent considerable time in the country, Stan. Personally, I've always liked his reporting. Just the facts!" Rosen said amiably.

Did the senator have an inkling about Arikos? Had he set this meeting up intentionally, Marc asked himself. He didn't want anything laid on the table yet.

Rosen listened quietly to Arikos' abrupt dismissal of the Saharan problem. "The Polisario are winning the war right now. Let them have the Sahara. It's theirs!"

Rosen's eyes shone. *He's weighing what I've told him*, Marc thought. But he was beginning to feel edgy. He had to get those papers out of the Senate building, pronto. The story on Arikos would never hold water if he didn't provide proof. He made an excuse about an urgent appointment.

Arikos' hand reached down to Marc's briefcase.

"Any hot telexes in here?" His voice was laced with venom. "Perhaps the senator would like to have a look at what came in last night."

He pressed the release on the clasp. It was locked.

"I don't carry around the latest communiqués, Mr. Arikos," Marc said, reaching for the case. Damnit! He seemed to know what was inside.

"So why lock it?" Arikos' jeering lip curled. His hand was still on the case.

"Just habit!" Marc wrenched the briefcase away and blurted apologies to Rosen.

The doorway was crowded with appointment-seekers. He turned and saw Arikos rise from the table, excusing himself. A group waited, blocking access to the elevators across from the dining room. Damn! Arikos knew the building better than he did. Where were the stairs? Where the nearest exit? He started toward the door to C Street, hundreds of yards away down a green marble tunnel, dizzyingly striated with black. He broke into a run, feeling himself submerged in a sea of kelp that was closing in on him. From the corner of his eye, he saw Arikos leaving the dining room. He darted down a hall to the right and into an open elevator. The building was on the side of a hill. There had to be another exit on the first floor. Emerging, he saw the door to Constitution Avenue and raced for it, colliding with several people.

A taxi was waiting. As he opened the door, he saw the driver's afro, the black moustache, the North African skin tint. Libyan?

Marc slammed the door and spun around. Moving into the street, he hailed another cab. He threw a ten-dollar note at the driver and gave the address of the wire service.

As the taxi rolled with the traffic along the broad avenue, he collapsed in the seat. The strain of the last few days was beginning to show. Chimeras at every turn! Had Arikos really been chasing him? The driver with the afro in the other cab could have been from any one of a number of countries.

Epilogue

Walk not on the earth exultantly, for thou canst not cleave the earth, neither shalt thou reach to the mountains in height.

— Koran, 17:37

"High-ranking State Department official caught in multi-million-dollar scam!"

Marc's story broke in Washington the day after he received the copies of the Maltese bank deposits from Pat Simmonds.

"Stathis Arikos, State Department's influential Special Assistant for Sahelian Affairs, allegedly bribed by Qadhafi to deceive U.S. Government. Arikos spends frequent vacations at a palatial villa paid for by the Libyan chief of state."

Photographs of the Renaissance façade vied with slick portraits of Stan Arikos for prominence on front pages from coast to coast. Lurid descriptions of parties at the palatial villa named a number of Libyan officers who had been accompanied by trollops from the streets of Valletta. The scandal that hit streets across the U.S. began to resound through Europe and North Africa.

Stan Arikos was discharged from government service. Charged with venality, he was awaiting indictment. Marc had kept his promise. Pat Simmonds' name was kept out of it, and she had another job now. Aysha Larosien was hired by the National Council on U.S.-

Arab Relations and assigned to the section dealing with the status of women.

Aysha and Marc had long discussions about what the whole affair had amounted to. Obviously, the State Department wasn't infallible, nor was our shrinking newsgathering service around the world. Foreign correspondents rarely set foot in developing countries except in times of crisis. In these days of fast communication, involving space satellites, bulky television equipment and electronically equipped offices, it was too costly to maintain correspondents in every capital of the world. Facts were often cleverly misinterpreted or manipulated to influence U.S. foreign policy decisions. At home, many elements conspired to obscure the truth—lobbies representing huge amorphous groups, the commercial interests of corporations and nations, and the petty interests of individuals. There were, as there always have been, malefactors waiting in the wings to take advantage of the uninformed.

The United States needed all its antennae out to make sense of events in far-flung corners of the world. No other nation had so much to gain and so much to lose, for whether we have wished to be involved or not, we have found ourselves forever enmeshed in the problems of other countries. Even the winds from the Sahara blew through our land from across the sea.

Marc rejoiced for Morocco. Capitol Hill would soon permit the sale of reconnaissance planes and helicopters, among other arms, to the Moroccans. Thus, a more equitable military balance might be achieved, and the balance of power in North Africa between conservative and socialist nations preserved, until an agreement between Algeria and Morocco could be reached and a referendum held in the Sahara.

He felt a pang of regret when he learned that El-Ouali Mustapha Sayed, Polisario Secretary General, had been killed while on a raid deep into Mauretania, shortly after Marc had seen him. A fiery but foolhardy revolutionary! Why did he, the virtual leader of the insurgents, accompany a risky venture into another country? With its strong backing by Algeria and Libya, the Polisario would survive without him, perhaps even win the war. The important thing was that—no matter what the outcome for the Sahara—Morocco would be able to hold its own.

As to the future, he would have to hold his own with Aysha, the unveiled woman of the desert, with her intelligence, her energy and her deep concerns. They were to be married in a month.

But she was not alone in her mission. Meanwhile, the influence of Muslim women coming out from under in many countries around the globe was already making itself felt in ever-changing times. There was hope, he thought, for a world where society in all its forms continued to evolve toward freedom

Printed in the United States
724700005B